A wife...

Not a wife, he told himself harshly. He'd be house sharing and he'd be acting, nothing more. And with what was at stake, maybe he could do it. Maybe it wouldn't mess with his life. It wasn't as if he'd have free time to spend sharing.

Sharing Jodie's life?

What was she thinking now?

They were pulling up at the dock. As he headed for the gangplank, he thought he'd done all he could.

He'd asked a woman to marry him. He'd asked Jodie to save lives.

He could only hope that the indecision, the concern he'd seen flash through those deep blue eyes meant that she cared.

But part of him was already thinking...if she cared...

For him?

Yeah, right. *Shove that thought right out of your mind*, he told himself. It was only if she didn't care, if neither of them cared, that this thing could possibly work.

Dear Reader,

Do you ever look at people on public transport and imagine their stories? I can't help myself—surely that's where all writers get their inspirations?

So, winter. A long train journey along Australia's southeast coast. A soggy sandwich, a tepid cup of tea and an empty car. A stop in a town not too far from a great surfing spot and a young woman boards the train. Maybe in her late twenties? She's tall and her long blond hair is bleached and tangled. She's wearing shorts, sandals, a puffer jacket—yep, it's cold. A backpack. A battered surfboard. She gives me a friendly wave, then sits and disappears into her own company.

And I'm left with my imagination. A loner. Surely smart, kind, with a killer smile? A doctor? Why not? Off heads my imagination... An itinerant doctor, following the surf, filling in as a locum where she can. Obviously, she'll have a backstory to break your heart.

Who could deserve this woman? Who could win her heart?

Maybe out there a young woman is opening this book and thinking...*I own a surfboard. I travel by train. Was that...?* If it is, I hope you've found your Seb, and that he deserves you.

Happy reading,

Marion Lennox

The Doctor's Billion-Dollar Bride

MARION LENNOX

HARLEQUIN®
MEDICAL ROMANCE™

Recycling programs
for this product may
not exist in your area.

ISBN-13: 978-1-335-59543-0

The Doctor's Billion-Dollar Bride

Harlequin Enterprises ULC
22 Adelaide St. West, 41st Floor
Toronto, Ontario M5H 4E3, Canada
www.Harlequin.com

Printed in U.S.A.

Marion Lennox has written over one hundred romance novels and is published in over one hundred countries and thirty languages. Her international awards include the prestigious RITA® Award (twice!) and the *RT Book Reviews* Career Achievement Award for "a body of work which makes us laugh and teaches us about love." Marion adores her family, her kayak, her dog and lying on the beach with a book someone else has written. Heaven!

Books by Marion Lennox

Harlequin Medical Romance

Paramedics and Pups

Her Off-Limits Single Dad

Pregnant Midwife on His Doorstep
Mistletoe Kiss with the Heart Doctor
Falling for His Island Nurse
Healing Her Brooding Island Hero
A Rescue Dog to Heal Them
A Family to Save the Doctor's Heart
Dr. Finlay's Courageous Bride
Healed by Their Dolphin Island Baby
Baby Shock for the Millionaire Doc

Visit the Author Profile page
at Harlequin.com for more titles.

To Sheila, my editor and my friend.

With thanks for so many years of friendship, of guidance, of skill, of empathy and of travel stories. On opposite sides of the globe, it's always felt like the best of teams.

Warmest of warm wishes for always,

Marion

CHAPTER ONE

'I'M SORRY, BUT we have no space in today's class. Maybe we can arrange a private lesson tomorrow?'

Dr Jodie Tavish's surfing classes were almost always full, and she loved teaching the island's kids. As one of Kirra Island's three doctors, Jodie's workload wasn't huge, and her Saturday morning classes were a way of passing on the skills she loved.

But the man demanding a lesson—right now!—wasn't a kid. He looked well into his eighties.

It might be fun to try and teach him though, Jodie thought, but unless he'd surfed before he'd need to accept his limits. He was wearing board shorts, and she surreptitiously checked out his legs—skinny and a bit shaky. If she got him to his knees she'd be lucky, and she'd need to run him through a medical checklist first, even if it did offend him.

From the way he was behaving, though, she suspected it would offend him, but she'd have to do it.

But it might never happen. Right now, she had kids waiting, and this angry man was blocking her path.

'I can pay more than any of these kids put together,' he barked. 'Someone else can teach them.

The woman at the resort says you're the best, and I want you.'

'I'm afraid you can't have me,' she said, still mildly. 'These kids have paid up front, and I can't take more than six. It's not safe.'

'Then give me a private lesson straight after.'

'I can't do that either. I'm a doctor and I have other commitments...'

'You're a doctor?'

'Yes, so I only do this part-time. If you'd like to put your name down for a private lesson to-morrow...'

'I'm going home tomorrow. I want a lesson now.'

'No. I'm sorry.'

And the man's anger seemed to escalate. 'Do you have any idea who you're turning down?' he demanded. 'I'm Arthur Cantrell, head of the biggest mining conglomerate in Australia. Tell these girls I'll pay them off—just get rid of them.'

Whoa.

'These girls have limited time too,' she told him, managing, with an effort, to keep her voice mild. 'They booked weeks ago. If you have so much money, I suggest you prebook and visit the island again.'

Enough. His colour was mounting but she turned away and headed for the group of teenage girls at the water's edge. The guy stood glaring after her, his anger palpable.

Kirra Island was becoming a popular destination for the wealthy since the opening of a health resort at the south end of the island. This guy must be at the upper echelons of the wealthy guest list, she thought. His face and upper neck were tanned, but the rest of him looked like it hadn't seen the sun for decades. Short and wiry, he had silvery hair and thick, bushy eyebrows. His voice had been crisp, authoritative, commanding. Aged or not, he'd look distinguished in a business setting.

There was a taxi sitting in the car park. Mack Henderson ran the only taxi on the island. It must have cost the guy heaps to hire Mack to wait, she thought, and idly wondered how much he had been prepared to pay.

But who cared? Normally, on a Saturday afternoon she could have squeezed in a private lesson, but not today. Today's date felt like a leaden weight in her heart—as this date had for the last fifteen years. After this lesson, unless medical imperatives intervened, she intended to surf by herself, surf until she was exhausted.

And right now her students were bouncing, eager to be in the water, desperate to learn. Teenage girls…

Hali would be fifteen today, she thought. Hali. The name meant *the sea*. Hali, her own precious daughter.

Probably she wasn't even named Hali any more. No! Now wasn't for thinking of the past, nor was it for thinking of obnoxious businessmen waving wads of money. This morning was for teaching the next generation the joy of surfing, the joy of the sea.

She just had to hope, to believe, that somewhere, somehow, someone was doing the same for Hali.

'He's on Kirra Island.'

'What on earth is he doing there?'

It had taken Dr Sebastian Cantrell's receptionist three hours to track his great-uncle down. Arthur Cantrell, corporate mogul, one of the richest men in Australia, had a serious heart condition. At eighty-six, after two major heart events, with implanted pacemaker and defibrillator, everyone knew he was living on borrowed time. Fiercely private, he lived alone in his ridiculously opulent mansion and refused to have staff stay over. On weekends there was no one there.

He had, though, as a concession to Seb's 'stupid concerns' as he termed them, agreed to a personal security alarm, as well as the over-the-top security devices he'd fitted to keep his fortune of antiquities safe.

'What's the point of keeping your valuables safe if you don't keep yourself safe?' Seb had asked. Arthur had reacted angrily, as he always did at what he termed Seb's interference, but he had had the personal alarm installed.

He therefore had a disc he was supposed to wear

around his neck. There was also a bedside control he was supposed to press every morning. If it wasn't pressed by nine, then the security firm rang to remind him. If Arthur didn't answer, they rang Seb. Which had happened an hour ago.

His uncle, though, had failed to press the control any number of times before, and Seb had six patients with complex problems on his list this morning. So he'd asked his receptionist to phone, and when Arthur still didn't answer she'd asked his housekeeper to check. She'd reported back that Arthur was away, but she didn't know where.

And now Beth had succeeded in tracking him down, though, he gathered, not without difficulty.

'There's a new resort just opened on Kirra Island,' she told him. 'Mr Cantrell's secretary says he's booked in over the weekend. He flew there by helicopter yesterday afternoon and Trevor's due to pick him up tomorrow.'

'Oh, well done,' Seb told her and grinned. 'I bet you didn't think when you took this job that tracking elderly great-uncles would be on your list.'

'He's a worry,' Beth conceded. 'You want to phone him?'

'Not in a million years. His blast would burst my eardrums, but if you would…can you give the resort a ring? Quietly give them my number in case of issues.'

'Of course—but why does he resent you worrying?' she asked curiously, and Seb shrugged.

'He hates anyone worrying.'

But as he headed for the next patient, he thought his great-uncle didn't just resent him worrying. He resented him *being*.

So why did *he* care about the old man? Why did he keep trying?

Because someone had to, he told himself. Arthur was the only family Seb had, and the opposite was true. If Seb didn't care, there was no one else, and what did it matter if the old man couldn't stand him?

For his father and grandfather's sake he'd do the right thing, he told himself. Even though most of the time what he'd most like to do was walk away.

'Jodie, sorry, I have to go.'

Halfway through the lesson, Ellie Cray, the oldest of her would-be surfers, had glanced towards the beach and seen her father. 'Mum and Dad are picking me up early. We're meeting Auntie Hazel from the ferry and going out for lunch. Sorry.'

She sounded sorry too. She'd just succeeded in tottering to a standing position and had caught two waves. With half an hour's class to go, she sounded like it was almost killing her to leave.

'Next Saturday?' she pleaded, and Jodie gave her a thumbs up. She had five more kids to concentrate on, and the surf was building.

'Dump your board past the high tide mark and have a lovely lunch,' she told her, and watched her safely to shore before turning her attention back to the other girls.

It was a great morning and they were doing brilliantly. The waves were long, cresting rollers, curling in nicely along the relatively shallow beach. As long as they stayed clear of the rocks at the end of the cove, where the current ran sideways, she could almost relax.

One of the kids—Maria, a pale-faced kid with a fierce determination to get out to the big waves—was having trouble. She was standing too far forward, nosediving every time. The others were practising knees to feet, knees to feet, in the shallower waves, so she could spend a little time with Maria.

But… 'Jodie!' It was Katie, at twelve one of her youngest, and the alarm in her voice brought Jodie's fast attention. She swivelled. The remaining girls were fine, but Katie was standing in the shallows, staring towards the cove's corner. 'That guy,' she called. 'The one you were talking to. He's taken Ellie's board.'

She looked—and her breath caught in her throat. Katie was right.

The guy—Arthur whoever—was in the water, right out at the back of the breaking waves. He was lying on the board, looking backwards, as if waiting for the right wave.

He must have had some experience to get the board out that far, Jodie thought incredulously. She wouldn't have thought he'd have the strength, but for the last few moments there'd been a period of calm. She and Maria had been waiting for a decent wave as well.

So now what was he doing? Waiting to surf in? She thought of his body, skinny, shaky. She knew lots of older surfers, but this guy had asked for lessons. If he wasn't experienced…surely he couldn't control a board in decent surf?

And he didn't know the dangers waiting for the unwary at that corner of the cove. Where she and her students were, the waves were long and even, foaming gently to the beach. In the corner though, where the cliffs rose to form a headland, the waves rose higher and stronger, and as they neared the shore the current pushed them into a curve. Instead of rolling to the sandy shore, they veered to crash against the rocks under the headland.

There was a sign on the beach path warning of the dangers. This guy, though, must have stalked straight past the sign on his way to confront her. And finally grabbed the board and headed away from her group.

Into peril.

'Hey!' She didn't know she could shout so loud, but she needed to shout louder. 'Yell at him!' she screamed to the girls when he didn't react. 'And stay together and get to the beach. Beach, now!'

They were great kids. One of the first things she instilled in her students was that if she yelled

'Beach' then that was where they went, as fast as possible. She'd never had to use the command in the two years she'd been on the island, but it was there... In case of accident? In case of shark? Or right now, in case of a geriatric would-be surfer who was obviously trying to kill himself. The girls were in no danger, but they were her responsibility and she wasn't about to risk them to save him.

But they were heading for the shore, yelling as they went. She'd talked to them about the dangers of this beach, in case they came here without her to practise. They knew the dangers of the corner. Five teenage girls could make a fair noise when they tried, and she blessed them for it.

But the guy wasn't hearing—deliberately or not. He was still lying on the board, letting the shallow waves roll under him. It'd feel great, Jodie thought, to lie out there in the sun...

But not there.

She hit the beach and ran.

In her peripheral vision she could see Mack, the taxi driver. He'd have been watching while waiting for his passenger, she thought, and Mack was a local. He knew the dangers even more than she did. He was in his sixties and overweight, but he was running down the track like the athlete he'd been as a teen.

Neither of them could get there fast enough.

The corner was deceptive. Calm, calm, calm—and then not calm. There'd been a set of maybe a dozen small swells, but further out Jodie could see the next set forming. Big ones. Who knew what caused the differential? She certainly didn't. All she knew was that a wave was surging in, building, cresting, almost breaking—and then finally it reached the man on the board.

Then, while she watched in horror, it picked up man and board as if they were driftwood. It toppled them over and over within a mass of white water, curving in to smash them onto the rocks on the shore.

'He's gone surfing.'

'What?' Seb had been checking a corneal ulcer. Ron Harvey had been hammering nails into roofing iron when a sliver of metal had flown up and pierced his eye. A week on, it was still touch and go as to whether he'd lose the eye, but he wouldn't if Seb could help it.

Ron had fallen from the ladder trying to descend after the accident. He'd suffered a broken leg and lacerations, so it had been a while until it had been realised there was iron still in the eye. The eye had therefore been inflamed and stained from the iron before Seb had seen it. The inflammation itself was a major issue. There was no way Seb could use a steroid until it had healed, but without a steroid it was a case of meticulous care, daily dressings and a whole lot of hope.

Today, though, the size of the ulcer had slightly

diminished. This wasn't the sort of work Seb had dreamed of, but it was satisfactory enough, and hope was front and foremost as Seb emerged from Ron's ward.

But now his bubble of hope was displaced by incredulity. He stared at Beth as if she had two heads. His great-uncle had gone surfing? 'You're kidding me, right?'

'That's what the receptionist at the resort told me,' she replied. 'She's obviously young—no rules instilled yet about guest privacy—and was on for a chat. She says your great-uncle's headed off for a surfing lesson.'

'A lesson…' That was slightly better.

Arthur had surfed in his youth, he thought, re-membering stories his father had told him of his grandfather and great-uncle. As kids they'd ap-parently surfed together, before Arthur had taken over the family business and focused on making his squillions.

As far as he knew though, Arthur hadn't surfed… since when? Since he was a kid? According to his grandfather, Arthur hadn't thought of anything but making money for at least fifty years.

So now, surfing with his heart condition, his failing knee joints, and all the rest…

And, for heaven's sake, maybe this was his fault. There'd been a heated exchange—very heated—a couple of weeks back, and surfing had come into the mix. Arthur had spent his life making money and now, in his eighties, was desperate for Seb to take his rightful place as heir to Cantrell Holdings. Or, as a last resort, to provide him with an heir who would.

'Do you think nothing of family?' he'd demanded. 'You're so damned obsessed...'

'I'm obsessed?' Seb had thrown back at him. 'All you think of is money. Show me you're interested in something else—take a holiday, do something besides obsessing about the wealth you never spend. The world you currently inhabit makes my skin crawl and I want no part of it. There must be something else you enjoy.'

So Arthur had gone...*surfing*?

'He'll be okay,' Beth said, seemingly mirroring his thoughts. 'The receptionist said the instructor's a local doctor. Apparently, she teaches surfing part-time, for fun, but she's an extremely competent doctor. I can't imagine she'll let him do anything unsafe.'

'Since when has he let anyone stop him doing what he wanted to do?' Seb growled, but he was reassured. And hell, his great-uncle wasn't a kid. If he wanted to kill himself, who was Seb to try and stop him?

But as he headed off to see his next patient, for some reason Beth's words stayed with him.

'Apparently, she teaches surfing part-time, for fun.'

Was there really a world out there where a doctor had space to…teach surfing for fun?

The sand stopped at the edge of the cove, becoming a rock shelf around the base of the headland. At low tide the shelf was a great place to sit and watch the power of the sea.

It was high tide now though, and there was shallow water over the rocks. Jodie ran, blessing the swim shoes she always wore. They gave her grip so she could head fast towards the edge of the shelf.

Mack paused momentarily at the edge of the shelf, staring down at his shoes, obviously taking a moment to weigh the pros and cons of ruining leather brogues. The fact that he came right on was testament to how scared he was. How scared they both were.

She reached the edge. The guy's wave had surged back but another was driving in. She had to take a couple of fast steps back or she risked being sucked in herself.

Then Mack was beside her, gripping her arm. 'Where?' he said hoarsely. 'Can you see?'

And then they did. They saw the surfboard first, smashing on the rocks as the wave slammed it down. Arthur was behind, a limp figure being tossed forward. Face down in the foam.

For a moment there was nothing they could do.

They watched in sick horror as a third wave came through... And receded.

Jodie stared out at the sea. The set was done, the sea stilled, at least a little. Here under the headland, it was never still, but still enough. It looked as if he was being washed into a crevice-like break in the shelf.

This was her only chance. She started forward but Mack gripped her arm. 'You can't...'

'If I'm fast.'

'Geez, Doc, the guy's crazy.'

'Yeah, but he's probably still alive.'

'There's a rope in the cab. I can...'

'You know there's no time. Mack, I can do this.' She hoped.

What she was thinking went against all lifesaving rules—or medical rules? *Keep yourself safe at all cost.* But she'd surfed since she was a teenager, climbing in and out of places like this to find the best swells. Besides, she had no responsibilities. If anything happened, there'd be a ripple of sadness on the island, but the ripples would settle and life would go on.

Which was the way she liked it.

All that, though, was a flash of self-knowledge, an instant appraisal of risk and consequences, and then she was pulling away from Mack's arm, stepping forward and slipping down into the water.

The place where she entered was a crevice between two outreaching fingers of rock. The whole crevice was currently a mass of foam, swells pushing in, surging out again and crashing back into the incoming waves.

Jodie, though, was good. Blessing her shoes, using them to stall herself from being washed against the rocks herself, she tried as best she could to balance herself against the wash of water, and then set herself to wait.

There was no way she could push out and try to find Arthur—that'd end in injury or worse to herself. She simply braced as best she could, dug her feet into niches in the rock, spread her arms—and hoped like hell that he'd be washed against her. If she could just hold on...

And then she found him—or rather he found her. His limp body crashed against her, shoving her sideways.

The rest was pure reflex. Somehow, she grabbed, and tugged him hard against her. The water was hauling him back but somehow, she held on. She'd got this far. Dammit, she wouldn't let go.

'You got him!' It was a triumphant shout from above. 'I'm here, Doc, hang on.'

And Mack was lying on the rocks above. He'd be lying in the washing water, but his weight must be stopping him from sliding in while the waves were small.

Please, no big ones...

Mack was leaning down, his arms outstretched,

hands reaching. 'Can you push him up? Go, Doc, a bit higher. Higher…' And then… 'Got him!'

And somehow, he managed it, grasping the old man by one arm, pulling him higher, then managing to lock his hands under both arms. He pulled, Jodie pushed as best she could, and then the weight lifted from her. Mack had him out of the water.

His hands came down again. 'Doc…'

'Look after him.'

'Not till you're out,' Mack yelled. 'Big 'un coming. Now!'

It was amazing what panic could do. Her feet found leverage as she grabbed his outstretched hands and somehow hauled herself up. And then both of them grabbed the limp old man under his arms, one on each side. There was no time for trained paramedic holds, no time to do anything but grab what they could. And then they were stumbling back over the rocks, out of reach of the next set of breakers that could surely have killed them all.

Saturday was usually light. With work finished for the day, Seb headed home. His townhouse overlooked Brisbane's South Bank, a park surrounding a gorgeous man-made riverside lagoon. He swam there every morning—hard. Pushing himself to the edge of his physical endurance helped keep some of the demons at bay—but not all.

What was happening in Al Delebe? Border

problems were flaring again. Were his people safe? More, what was happening in the camps being set up for the displaced? He knew the camps well, dust bowls where the sweeping sands played havoc with eyes.

Why was he here?

He'd finally accepted the reason, but he didn't have to like it, and the voices in his head gave him no relief. His parents' voices, and his grandfather's, had instilled the same mantra since childhood.

'You're on this earth to do good, Seb...'

He could do so much more if he...

No. *If* wasn't possible. What he was doing was useful. Just not as useful as he needed it to be.

So cut it out with the guilt, he told himself, and for some reason he found himself thinking of his great-uncle.

And then, stupidly, he was thinking of the woman Beth had mentioned in passing.

'Apparently, she teaches surfing part-time, for fun, but she's an extremely competent doctor.'

A doctor who practised medicine on a tiny subtropical island, he thought, probably attaching herself to a fancy wellness resort for the rich and indulged. A woman who had space in her life to surf in her spare time. What sort of life would that be?

He'd accused his great-uncle of living a life that

made him cringe, but in truth Seb's life was also driven.

For a moment he imagined himself in such a life—a little medicine, nothing hard, then surfing in his spare time.

A life where the voices in his head let him off the hook?

It wasn't going to happen, he told himself, and the guilt kicked in even as he thought about it. But just for a moment, the voices faded and an almost primeval urge took over.

It was a great afternoon and a Saturday. Maybe *he* could surf. Or try to surf. His sole experience was as a teenager, staying with a mate from boarding school over the summer break. He had managed to stand, to catch some smallish waves. It was a fleeting memory but it was a good one.

So... It was Saturday afternoon and there was decent surf less than an hour's drive away. Maybe he could leave the mass of paperwork ensuing from his latest fundraising drive, and the preparation for the speech he'd promised at a charity ball next week. There'd surely be a place he could hire a board.

But back they came, the voices.

Surf? How would that help? How many people's vision depended on him? The voices were a hammering at the back of his head.

He sat down at his desk, pulled up his computer files and stared at the screen.

But the thought didn't fade. A doctor who surfed… For some reason the image was messing with his head.

And then he was thinking of Arthur, probably attempting a surfing lesson right now. Ridiculously. With his heart it'd be crazy.

But then he thought, why not? At eighty-six, what did Arthur have to lose? Maybe at eighty-six his great-uncle could finally change?

As if.

He stared at the screen a bit longer but his fingers stayed still. Maybe he was turning into a version of Arthur? Sure, his compulsion was his charity, whereas Arthur's was making money, but for some reason Arthur had taken time off and gone surfing.

'And I'm thirty-six,' Seb said out loud. 'Am I going to wait fifty years for my turn?'

But…

Enough.

'But nothing,' he told the voices. Then he slammed the lid closed on his computer and headed out to find some waves.

CHAPTER TWO

THIS HAD TO happen when Misty and Angus were off the island.

Normally Kirra Island had three doctors, but Misty and Angus were married with kids, and they'd taken this weekend off.

Six weeks back a tropical storm had crashed across the island, causing untold damage. The fishing fleet had been decimated and houses damaged. With so much destruction there'd been an ongoing stream of injuries as islanders fought to clear debris and make repairs. The minor injuries that entailed meant that for weeks the three part-time doctors had become almost full-time.

Now though, with demands easing and with Misty in the first stages of pregnancy, both Angus and Misty were anxious to take a break and spend time with their little family. They were therefore in Brisbane, which meant Jodie was stuck as the only doctor. So now…she was grazed and bruised, and she'd really like to go home to her snug little cottage and whinge for her country. Instead, she was stuck in Kirra's tiny clinic-cum-hospital, making sure an old man didn't die on her watch.

He should have been airlifted to Brisbane.

Once they'd got him out of the water, they'd called for reinforcements. Martin, the island's nurse-cum-paramedic—had brought the island ambulance. Parents had arrived to pick up kids.

Thankfully, the old man had revived without CPR. His most obvious injury, apart from a mass of minor lacerations and bruises, was a broken arm.

That might well have been from where she and Mack had grabbed him, she'd thought as she'd examined him, but there'd been no choice. They'd been lucky not to have fractured his scapula and clavicle—she'd been relieved to see only a minor break to the humerus. She'd started antibiotics to prevent lung infection, she'd stabilised his arm and she had him propped up on pillows. So far, so good.

His heart, though, was a different matter. His blood pressure on admission was over two hundred, and the tell-tale bulge on his shoulder wasn't caused by the break.

It was caused by an implant.

She got answers to her questions in monosyllabic grunts. He had a pacemaker? An implanted defibrillator? 'Yes.' What heart events in the past? 'Two. Minor stuff. They made a damned fuss.'

Right, she'd thought, almost thankfully. This warranted immediate transfer to Brisbane—she'd call a medevac chopper straight away. But when she'd told him what she intended, she got more than grunts. With painkillers on board, he obviously felt strong enough to blast again.

'You can call anyone you like, but I'm not getting into any ambulance. I'll refuse and you can't make me—I'll have you up for assault if you try. Get the taxi to take me back to the resort, woman, and leave me be. Trevor's coming with the chopper tomorrow. He'll take me home.'

Really? What was the likelihood they'd put him to bed and one of the resort's cleaning staff would find him dead in the morning? High enough to make the idea impossible.

'That can't happen,' she'd said briskly. 'The resort won't accept you. You're not going back to Brisbane without accompaniment either. Trevor's the helicopter pilot? If he's at the controls, there's nothing he can do if you have a heart event. You do understand the risk? Mr Cantrell, who can we call? A relative? A friend?'

She'd got a death stare for her pains. 'I'm fine on my own. Take me back to the resort. You don't have to tell them what's happened.'

'That's not an option,' she'd said, because he might be stubborn but she'd dealt with cantankerous patients before. 'And you *will* need help to return to the mainland. This Trevor, I assume he's a commercial pilot? He needs to know the facts and it's our responsibility to give them to him.'

If anything, the death stare had intensified, but she'd gazed blandly back. With effort. The last thing she wanted was to keep this guy here. Medically, she was by herself tonight. With his history he needed to be in ICU, or at least having hourly obs. Her fingers were itching to ring for evacuation. But…

'I won't go,' he said fretfully. 'I refuse.'

'Then give me a name—someone we can call.' Mack had already been through his wallet and found no emergency contact details.

He glared but she glared back.

'Fine,' he said at last. 'Ring my great-nephew. As far as I'm concerned, he's a waste of space but he'll come if I tell him to.'

But he hadn't. She'd rung the number she'd been reluctantly given—for a Sebastian Cantrell—and the phone had rung out. She'd rung three times, left messages each time, and nothing. Arthur had refused to give her another number.

So finally, she'd taken the only option. She'd settled Arthur into one of the two beds in the island's clinic-cum-hospital and settled herself to wait the night out. This Trevor was coming in the morning, so maybe Martin could go with him and take the ferry back. If Arthur refused to go to hospital once he was on the mainland, that was his business, but tonight, bruised, battered and his blood pressure still dangerously high, sending him anywhere without medical support was impossible.

The clinic's two beds were used for islanders with minor needs, an islander with gastro who needed rehydration, or one of the island's elderly, shaken after a fall but not hurt enough to need the stress of transfer to the mainland.

Usually, Martin stayed with them overnight, but tonight Jodie's attendance was the closest thing she could organise to intensive care. But this was a clinic, not a hospital. There were no state-of-the-art monitors to alert her if there was a cardiac falter, so she had to stay close.

Oh, but she was so sore, and oh, she wanted her own bed. And in the background there was still the nagging knowledge of what day this was. To say she was feeling wretched would be an understatement.

And at nine, while she was sitting beside Arthur's bed, growing grumpier by the minute, finally her phone rang.

'Dr Tavish?' The voice sounded smooth, assured, completely unapologetic. 'This is Sebastian Cantrell. I believe I've missed your call.'

'You've missed three.' Dammit, she hadn't meant to sound peevish but she couldn't help herself. She'd wrenched her own shoulder pulling his great-uncle over the rocks, and it had hurt as she'd lifted the phone.

'I apologise.' He didn't sound sorry though. He sounded irritated. 'I've been surfing. Is there a problem with my great-uncle?'

He'd been surfing? Salt in the wound, she thought. Arthur had described him as *'a waste of space'*, and right now she was prepared to accept the descriptor without argument.

'Your uncle tried surfing too,' she told him. 'Unfortunately, he surfed into rocks.' She glanced at Arthur and saw he was awake, so switched her phone to speaker. 'He's beside me now, hearing this conversation. Arthur, do I have your permission to tell your nephew your condition?' She got a hazy nod—painkillers were making the old man drift in and out of sleep. 'Your uncle agrees,' she said into the phone. 'We have him in our small clinic-cum-hospital. He has a fractured arm and lacerations. Plus...'

'Plus his heart condition.' The voice at the end of the line was incredulous. 'Are you the doctor who does the surfing lessons? You let him surf *near rocks*?'

Deep breath. *Don't lose it too*, she told herself, though she was pretty close.

'Your uncle wasn't under my supervision at the time.'

'But he was with you?'

For heaven's sake, what was he implying? A lawsuit?

'Could we leave this discussion for another time? All that matters now is that he needs evacuation to Brisbane, but he's refusing medevac.'

'He needs medevac. Do you know how dicey his heart is?' The incredulity was still there.

'I don't have a full history but I'm assuming...'

'Don't assume,' he snapped. 'Brisbane Private will send you a history.'

'Not without his permission, which I don't have.'

'You have mine. I have medical power of attorney.'

She looked down at Arthur and got a scowl and a fierce shake of his head. 'My medical history is my business,' he hissed, but he'd already told her that.

So… 'Not while he's conscious and mentally fine,' she said into the phone. But even if she got the history, it wouldn't do her any good. She hadn't the equipment or the skills to deal with the complex cardiac conditions this man obviously had.

'Put him on,' Seb snapped. 'He has to agree.'

But once again Arthur was shaking his head. 'Tell him to get stuffed,' he managed. 'Or…you can tell him to come and get me in the morning. My secretary will give him Trevor's number. He can come with the chopper—that'll fix your stupid edict that I need a nursemaid. And you…' he raised his voice, presumably so Sebastian could hear without Arthur having to take the phone '…you might as well make yourself useful. This stupid woman won't let me go back to the mainland without someone holding my hand. I'll see you in the morning.' And then he closed his eyes and refused to say another word.

'Dr Tavish?' The voice on the end of the phone now sounded resigned.

'Yes.' She was so over the pair of them.

'I'll have to organise a few things but I will come and get him.'

'That's big of you.' Whoa, that was hardly a professional response, but weariness and pain were both kicking in—being bashed onto rocks had left her with enough bruises and scratches to make even the second bed in her little clinic look good.

'What time?' the voice snapped, and she thought *like uncle, like nephew.*

'The earlier the better,' she snapped back. 'I'll endeavour to keep him alive until then, but it would be wise to have medical assistance on the chopper.'

'So you accept there's risk?'

'We don't have a cardio unit here. I'd like him gone tonight but he won't accept it. Of course there's risk. I can't call medevac just to have him refuse to board.'

'What about private medical evacuation? There is a service. He can afford it and it's his money down the drain if he refuses.'

Whoa. Private medical evacuation? A chopper full of trained medical staff? Did he have any idea how much that would cost? And now…the old man was glowering, his anger building. At this rate he'd work himself into a heart event, she thought.

'He won't go,' she said, stepping in before what looked like an imminent explosion, and that created a pause.

'I guess it's his choice,' he said at last. 'And if he dies before morning...'

'I've told him there's a chance, but he's refused. I can only hope he doesn't.'

'Because it'd mess with your surfing, you mean?' he demanded.

What a toerag. He was trying to turn the tables on her, put the guilt on her?

Enough. 'I'm disconnecting,' she said, just as coldly. 'Goodnight.'

'I told you.' As she disconnected, Arthur was almost spitting invective. 'He's not the least bit interested in me or what I care about. Nothing but his own stupid passions. He inherited family money— money earned from *our* company, our *family* company. But there's no sense of family responsibility. It's a wonder he's even in the country. He spends Cantrell money heading off to godforsaken countries, all of it useless...'

'He's coming to get you,' she said mildly.

'Only because you stood up to him. Good for you, girl.'

'Don't soft-soap me,' she retorted. 'All I did was tell him what a pig-headed relative he has in you. Family is family, it seems, and he's coming. But Arthur, honestly, you'd be much better off in Brisbane. I've explained. You know it's not safe to stay here.'

'I'm over being safe,' he told her. 'Eighty-six

and a heart that seems twenty years older. I should have died today.'

'Did you want to die?' she asked curiously, and he shook his head.

'Not before I've pulled my fool of a nephew into line. All I wanted was a surfing lesson.'

'So stealing a surfboard—you'll be billed for that, by the way—was a way of punishing me? You'll be pleased to know you succeeded.'

She was wearing a skirt and blouse—the change of clothes she always left at the clinic. Martin had stayed on while she'd had a fast shower, but she wasn't exactly looking her professional best. Now she lifted her leg to show a mass of grazing down her left calf, from being bashed against the rock shelf. 'Take a look at this,' she ordered. 'Yes, yours is worse, but without Mack and me…'

And that caused a pause. He stared down at the mass of scratches and bruises on her leg and his face twisted. Anger faded and suddenly he sounded older. Exhausted. Even guilty?

'You dived in. I thought… Was it *you* who pulled me out?'

'For what it's worth, yes.'

'It's worth a bit,' he said, closing his eyes again. 'I didn't think…but today on the beach, when I was hurtling towards those rocks… It makes a man think.'

'Does it make a man think he ought to go to Brisbane?'

'Maybe tomorrow,' he said wearily. 'I'll sleep now.'

'Good idea,' she said, suddenly gentle. He really had had a close call. 'As long as your heart keeps ticking, then you'll be fine.'

'And you'll stay?'

What choice did she have?

'I'll stay.'

'Good girl,' he said, and he finally gave in to the effects of shock and drugs and plain old age— and slept.

She borrowed the pillows from the second clinic cubicle, propped them on the wall and tried to doze in the chair.

Which wasn't exactly possible.

Firstly, it wasn't safe for her to sleep deeply. Given her druthers, she'd have taken a bucketload of painkillers herself and curled up on the spare bed, but Arthur did need watching. Specialling, they'd called it during her training—a nurse would sit with high-risk patients all night.

But nurses would watch in shifts. In a hospital setting one person wasn't rostered to watch all night, especially when that one person was as sore as she was.

Maybe she should have called Angus and Misty to come home, she thought. They could have caught the last ferry. But they hadn't had time off for so long, and they'd planned on taking Forrest, their nine-year-old, to the Brisbane Carnival tomorrow.

Which was actually today, Jodie realised, as midnight came and went, but then she thought of Forrest, excited beyond belief at the thought of the carnival. And Misty and Angus—and toddler Lily—Forrest's family…

What had she said to Arthur tonight? *Family is family.* Forrest had had a tough beginning but now he had parents who adored him, a baby sister he loved, a Gran, a dog, family.

And there were those thoughts again. Thoughts of Hali. Her baby. Fifteen today.

No, fifteen yesterday. She'd missed her birthday. Yet again.

And whether it was the culmination of a horrible day, the shock, the pain and the sheer discomfort of what she was doing now, or whether it was those memories flooding back—surely, they should have stopped by now, but maybe they never would—suddenly she found she was grabbing tissues from the bedside cabinet and disappearing behind them.

And when she emerged, Arthur was awake, looking at her in the dim light cast by the night lamp.

'Do you have a cold?' he growled. 'Oh, great. Contagious? That's all I need.'

'I don't have a cold,' she managed, and there was a long silence.

It was the strangest atmosphere, sitting in this silent clinic. Maybe it was getting to him too, for when he spoke again the gruffness had gone from his voice.

'So…crying? Why?'

'I don't cry.'

'Bull,' he growled. 'Men troubles? No, don't tell me, it's always men troubles.'

'It isn't men troubles. My leg hurts.'

He winced at that, and swore, but then his gaze intensified. 'Okay, I'm sorry, but crying? I still don't buy it. Want to tell Uncle Arthur why?'

As if. 'You're my patient, not my uncle,' she told him. 'Do you need more painkillers?'

'Do you?' He glanced down towards her leg.

'I'm on duty. We're talking about you.'

That produced another long look. Assessing? 'I am grateful you saved my life,' he said reluctantly. 'I still have people to annoy, a nephew to bring into line. But I wouldn't mind painkillers.'

Great. She could be a doctor again instead of a confidante. She busied herself, checking his blood pressure—still way too high—organising meds and wishing she had staff to check dosages. She was tired and she hurt, and there were still these emotions…

They had to be ignored. Drugs administered, she settled back in her chair and hoped Arthur would go back to sleep. But he was still watching her.

'So…crying?'

Oh, enough. 'That's none of your business.'

'I know,' he said bluntly. 'But I wouldn't mind knowing. It seems you saved my life so if there's anything I can do… Fix money troubles? Organise a hitman to take out a lowlife causing you grief?'

And at that she even managed a smile. 'Thank you, but honestly, I have no one to hit.' And then curiosity got the better of her. 'Could you really do that?'

'I'd have no idea how,' he admitted. 'But I have contacts and wealth. I dare say I could organise it.'

'So you can organise anything?'

'Not everything,' he said and glowered. 'Blasted family.'

'Your nephew?'

'You got it. Ungrateful brat.'

'He doesn't sound like a brat,' she said cautiously. 'He sounds like a grown man.'

'He's a brat. Do you know how extensive the Cantrell mining group is? How much power's behind it? He's due to inherit, but off he goes, flibbertigibbeting from country to country, getting into trouble, mixing himself up with all these exotic diseases, caring for nothing but himself…'

'Flibbertigibbeting?' she asked faintly.

'Just stuff and nonsense,' he snapped, anger growing again. 'Wasting his inheritance, spending money like water, doing whatever he wants. He's just like you, only at least you have the decency to save the odd life. The boy's the only family I have, and I might as well have none.' He glowered again and then fixed her with a stare. 'So that's me. What about you? Do you have family?'

'I… No,' she said, caught off-guard, and the old man's eyes narrowed. Homing in for the kill?

'So you're crying because?'

And what was there about the night, the pain, the weariness—and the sheer effort she'd have to make to deflect him—that made her say…

'Because I don't have a family. Yesterday was my daughter's birthday, but I lost her fifteen years ago.'

'You lost your daughter? What do you mean? How?'

She caught herself at that. What on earth was she saying? She never talked about Hali. Her daughter was her business.

No, she wasn't. Hali had stopped being her business fifteen years back.

But Arthur was still at it. Maybe he was using her to drive away his own pain and shock. Whatever, he wasn't letting up.

'Fifteen years back,' he muttered, staring at her. 'You must have been a kid yourself.'

'I was fifteen,' she said, and could have bitten her tongue out for saying it. Where was her head?

'Your parents?'

'I haven't seen them for years. Mr Cantrell, please…'

'So you're as alone as me then,' he said, bitterness returning to his voice. 'I bet you'd like a family who cares.'

And that was a gut punch. There was a long silence until finally she spoke again.

'I guess I would,' she told him. 'But you have… what did you call him…a flibbertigibbet nephew, and I have my work and my surfing and my colleagues. Mr Cantrell, I don't know why I said that. What I just told you was private. Could I ask you to respect that?'

'I've got no one to gossip to,' he told her. 'No wife to whinge to. No family to put up with me. So we're two of a kind and I respect that. But it's time you stopped crying.' And then his voice turned bleak. 'Families just let you down, over and over, and the sooner you accept you're better without them, the better you'll be.'

'But you're still trying with your nephew?'

'Fat chance I have of succeeding,' he muttered. 'I'd need a miracle.'

And then, to her relief, he closed his eyes. Conversation done.

CHAPTER THREE

THE NEPHEW FLEW in at nine the next morning, on board Arthur's private chopper. It landed on the stretch of land between the clinic and the sea. Jodie was at the window, watching as it landed. The pilot stayed aboard. The other occupant—the flibbertigibbet?—strode up towards the clinic like a man on a mission.

He was tall and lean—very lean—with dark brown hair and bronzed skin. Wearing fawn-coloured chinos and the sleeves of his open-necked shirt rolled up, he was striding fast, looking like he had no time to waste.

Well, neither did she. As long as nothing else happened on the island, the moment Arthur left she could go home and sleep. It was Sunday and Angus and Misty would be home later this afternoon. Maybe she could sleep for twenty-four hours?

She headed out to Reception to meet him. 'Mr Cantrell?'

'It's Dr Cantrell,' he said, almost a snap, making it obvious he was not here to waste time. His face looked set and grim. 'You can call me Seb.'

But she was still processing the first statement. 'Doctor?' This didn't fit with Arthur's description. 'Um…philosophy?'

'Medicine,' he said curtly, seemingly annoyed. 'I'm an ophthalmologist.'

'Really?' An eye specialist? That was so far away from his uncle's description of him as a wastrel that she could only stare.

'I know,' he said, still grim. 'Arthur will have told you I'm useless, and I am to him. Maybe I am to myself as well, but that's another story. Regardless, I have enough medical knowledge to safely escort him back to Brisbane. I've booked him into South Brisbane Private—that's the only hospital luxurious enough to cater for his whims, and it also has access to emergency cardio if needed. I assume he's stable now? Good, let's get him moved.'

Whoa. A one-minute handover? But if he was a doctor, and if he knew his uncle's history, hooray, they could both go.

But for some reason he'd paused and now he was looking down at her leg.

The skirt she'd changed into the night before was knee-length, slightly flared. It was what she left at the hospital because when she needed it— which was seldom—it was usually at a time when she was stressed and needed something light.

She hated wearing scrubs—in truth, she and Misty and Angus had made the decision not to wear them unless they were dealing with something really messy. *The islanders should see us as normal people, not medical machines,'* Misty had decreed. *'They'll treat us better that way.'*

So now she was wearing a light skirt, a floral blouse and…okay, theatre clogs. Somehow, her beach shoes had disappeared into the surf the day before.

But it wasn't the clogs Seb was looking at. Her left leg was exposed from the knee down. She'd washed it the night before and applied a liberal coating of antiseptic. The brown of the antiseptic had mingled with the weeping abrasions, making her leg look a bloody mess.

'Ouch,' he said, frowning. 'Did you both hit rocks?'

'Yeah,' she muttered. 'I'll take you in to your uncle.'

But he reached out and gripped her shoulder, stopping her turning away. 'There are things I don't understand. You're hurt? Because of my uncle?'

This was weird. He was holding her in a grip that was strong and sure, searching her face, his eyes creased into concern. As if he…cared? And for some dumb reason the sensation was doing her head in.

Oh, for heaven's sake, this feeling was just because she was tired. She did hurt, and there'd been no one, but there'd always been no one. Why was she suddenly feeling like she wanted to sink into this man's grip and let herself savour the strength of him?

This was dumb. She did not need this.

She did not need anyone.

'I'm fine,' she managed, trying to pull back. 'It's your uncle who needs the care. I've written up as detailed a medical report as I can. Do you have a defibrillator on board? His blood pressure's lowered but it's still of concern.'

'I won't need a defibrillator,' he said but he didn't release her shoulders. 'He has one fitted.'

Damn. How stupid was she? Basic medicine. If Arthur's heart faltered, the implants would do what an external machine would do.

She flushed. 'I know that. Sorry,' she muttered, but he was still reading her face. Questioning.

'You're exhausted.'

'It's been a long night.'

'What else has happened?'

'Nothing,' she snapped, and it was impossible to stop the weariness coming through. 'But I couldn't leave your uncle.'

'You don't have backup? Nursing staff?'

'Not this weekend.'

'So you slept here?' He sounded incredulous.

'If you could call it sleeping. Arthur's through here.'

Once again, she tried to pull back but his hands still held.

'The grazes… How…?'

'I pulled him out of the sea,' she said, goaded. For heaven's sake, what was happening here? Why was she being held? She just wanted to get rid of the pair of them and get some sleep. 'If you want to know, my surf class was full, your uncle was angry I wouldn't take him so he stole one of my surfboards. Then he went into one of the most dangerous places to surf on the island and was immediately washed onto rocks. I had to go in after him. Our local taxi driver helped me haul him out, but for a while it was touch and go.'

'The driver dived in, too?'

'Mack has more sense,' she said. 'All of us in the water? We're not idiots. Anyway, your uncle lost consciousness, but only momentarily. He's broken his arm—I have that strapped. I've started antibiotics and kept him on IV fluids plus intravenous pain meds. His lungs will need to be checked on the mainland, as will the lacerations he's received. We have a transport stretcher—can you and your pilot help move him? I can call our nurse if I must, but on a Sunday morning I won't call Martin in unless it's really necessary.'

That brought a moment's silence, loaded with incredulity. He let go of her shoulders and stood back, staring at her in disbelief.

'He washed onto rocks—yet you dived in?'

'There wasn't a choice,' she said bitterly. 'The punishment for stupidity and arrogance shouldn't be death.'

'He's eighty-six.'

'So you wouldn't have dived in?'

'I probably would, but he's my uncle.'

'So why weren't you there watching? Someone should be looking after him.'

And that brought more silence. He raked his hair, his long fingers pushing through already unruly deep brown waves. She thought suddenly, his face was almost too thin, too drawn. He looked... as tired as she was?

Or maybe not. A different form of tired?

A tiredness that seemed bone-deep.

'I do my best,' he said at last. 'But he's not... family.'

There was that word again. Family. That sounded like a rabbit hole she had no intention of heading down. It was not her place to care for the two of them.

'Fair enough,' she said. 'Let's get him transferred.' Oh, the thought of them both leaving. She might not even make the effort to walk back to her own little house. She might just sink onto the spare clinic bed and sleep right here.

But then the phone rang. The clinic phone. Her own phone buzzed at the same time.

Work.

Medical calls came through to the clinic, but they were also directed to the private phone of the doctor on call. This synchronised ring meant this was a medical call, and at the weekend the islanders knew only to call in cases of real need. She sighed, glancing longingly through at the spare bed, but she had no choice but to answer.

'Excuse me,' she told Seb and turned away.

Her last call on the desk handset had been to a pharmacy supplier, and she'd been left on hold for fifteen minutes. Therefore, the phone was still on speaker, which meant the man's voice at the other end came through as clearly as if he was in the room.

'Doc?' She heard the immediate anxiety. 'It's Cliff Michaels.'

She knew Cliff—he and his wife ran a surf shop in Kirra's little township. 'Hey, Cliff. What's the problem?'

'It's Ruby. She and her mates decided to build a cubby. Seems they found a sheet of tin, blown off from somewhere during the storm. They got into my shed and got nails. She's thumped a nail into tin and something's slivered off. Gone into her eye. She's in real trouble, Doc. A lot of pain and there's bleeding. Can I bring her in?'

'Of course,' she told him, and had to suppress the urge to groan. There went her chance of sleep. 'I'm at the clinic now. Bring her right in.'

She disconnected and sighed.

She turned and found Seb was now looking at her with speculation. That impression, that he was somehow reading her thoughts, seemed to intensify.

'So…' he said slowly. 'Lacerated eye?'

'Yeah,' she said wearily. 'Ruby's ten, a tough little kid. If Cliff says she's in trouble, then she really is. If it's serious… I'll do what I can but she'll probably need to go to Brisbane.' She frowned, thinking forward. 'I'd ask you to take her back with you, but I'm not sure yet about her flying. There's a ferry at midday…'

'I can help.'

'*Really?*' She hadn't meant that to sound like it did—as if the thought of him being useful was absurd. His uncle's attitude must have embedded itself, she thought. But then…if he truly was an ophthalmologist…

'Your uncle needs transfer,' she said.

'I understand that' he told her, still watching her face. 'But Arthur's choice was to wait here overnight, so unless things are deteriorating, he might as well wait another hour. Are things deteriorating?'

'I… No.'

'Well, there you go then,' he told her and he smiled. And that smile…

It changed his face. He'd been looking questioning, but before that he'd seemed grim, angry that his weekend had just been interrupted by an idiot uncle. His initial approach, a man in a hurry to get this over with, had left her with a feeling of distaste. But this smile…it changed things. It made him seem…gentle? Kind?

How could one smile do that? And why was it making her feel…like she didn't understand what she was feeling?

'I know what my uncle thinks of me and maybe he's right,' he was saying. 'But just occasionally my qualifications come in handy. It seems I'm in the right place at the right time, and maybe I owe you. Maybe my uncle and I both owe you. So I'll go see him and tell him we need to pay a debt, and if things seem stable then he can wait a bit longer. Then I need to see what equipment you have. Right, Dr Tavish, let's deal with Ruby together.'

Arthur might consider his great-nephew a waste of space, but five minutes after Ruby's arrival Jodie was having a serious rethink.

Ten-year-old Ruby was a wiry, scrappy kid, one of the gang of island kids who travelled as a pack. Her parents' surf-hire business right on the beach made the Michaelses' home a base for most of them.

Jodie had met Ruby a few times before, and it was mostly for trauma, falling out of trees, slicing her leg on the fin of a surfboard, cutting her feet on shells. Normally she arrived blasé—even belligerent—her attitude was that injuries were a nuisance, and her parents had no right to mess with her day by dragging her to the doctor—but today she came in huddled against her dad, holding a cloth to her eye, looking bedraggled and scared.

'Hey,' Seb said, before Jodie could introduce him. He stooped so he was on eye level with the child. 'You're Ruby? I'm Seb and I'm an eye doctor. It's a fluke that I'm here visiting Dr Jodie when you've hurt your eye. I'm guessing it must be hurting a lot, so the first thing we need to do is give you something to make you feel better. Then we need to fix it. Can we pop you up on the couch so Doc Jodie and I can take a look?'

It was exactly the right approach, direct, reassuring, positive. Cliff lifted his daughter onto the couch and Ruby's tough little persona reacted to Seb's direct approach. Where most kids would cry and cling, Ruby sank onto the pillows and calmly waited for him to follow through.

And he did. The lid of her left eye was lacerated, still sluggishly bleeding, but the deep scratch—and the pain—showed something had gone past the eyelid.

Ruby wasn't the most voluble kid. Jodie had expected to have trouble drawing her out, but Seb did it in minutes.

'So what sort of a cubby are you making?' he asked as he worked. 'I used to make big ones when I was a kid. I spent a lot of time overseas, in a place called Al Delebe. When I was about your age my mates found a hole at the back of our local rubbish dump, and we found all sorts of cool stuff. We never found enough iron for a proper roof, though. We used an old mattress once—it took four of us to drag it home. We propped it up on bricks. It made a great roof until we had a thunderstorm with really heavy rain. The whole thing collapsed and stuffing went everywhere. We had to admit where we'd got it from, and Dad had to hire a trailer and pay to take it back to the dump. We all had to help collect the stuffing. Boy, was I in trouble.'

And he had Ruby fascinated.

He had Jodie fascinated as well.

With Cliff sitting nervously in the background, close enough for Ruby to know her dad was near, Seb was doing a careful examination, with Jodie assisting.

Their little clinic was well equipped, and Seb had done a thorough check of what they had while they'd waited for Ruby to arrive. He'd also incidentally queried Jodie on what she was comfortable with him doing and what she could do herself. Now there was no hesitation.

He was wearing loupes, the specialist magnifying eye glasses they kept in their well-stocked equipment store. In between chatting—and Ruby was relaxing enough to chat—he had her focusing on a particular point in the ceiling. 'Dr Jodie will waggle her fingers above my head. Can you count how many fingers she's holding up? Now I'm just going to ask her to gently, very gently, hold your eyelids apart so you don't blink on me. Patients always blink. Can you try not to?'

And then… 'Yep, I see it. It looks like a tiny sliver of metal. It must have bounced up when you hit the tin. Wow, Ruby, you must have hit that nail really hard. Good arm muscles, huh? But the good news is that it doesn't seem to have gone into the inner eye—the part of your eye that makes you see.'

He looked for a little longer, checking and re-checking until he was sure he'd seen enough. Then he sat back, motioning Jodie to release Ruby's eye. 'Okay, team, we need to talk,' he said, and in those six words he'd pulled Cliff, Ruby and Jodie into a shared consultation.

Most doctors wouldn't do this, Jodie thought. They'd leave the room, take the parent outside, talk to their colleague separately. But Seb…this was some bedside manner.

'The sliver doesn't seem too deep but it's still a bit deep for me to tweezer it out,' he told them, and he was looking at Ruby as he spoke. Treating her like an adult. 'And also, where it is…it's important for us to get it out as fast as we can. It looks sharp and we don't want it working its way in further. Ruby, we could send you to Brisbane but that'll waste time. Luckily, I'm a specialist eye doctor and I can do it here. I've given you a painkiller—you're probably already feeling a bit better—right? That's great but pulling the sliver out might hurt a bit more. If Dr Jodie agrees, what

I think should happen is that we use more of the anaesthetic and make you sleepy.'

'Ruby had an anaesthetic six months back when she cut her feet on oyster shells,' Jodie told him. That was an accident that happened often on Kirra—surfers ending up on the oyster beds. The damage to their feet was often extensive and needed rigorous cleaning, so with nervous kids, or even some adults, a light general anaesthetic was often the way to go.

'So you'll know the process,' Seb said cheerfully. 'I give you a pinprick in your arm, the stuff in the needle will let you go to sleep for a few minutes, and I can pull out the sliver without you feeling a thing. Dr Jodie will help me. Is that okay with you, Ruby? Okay with you, Cliff?'

It seemed it was fine. So, twenty minutes later, with Cliff settled beside Arthur with instructions to call if needed—Kirra locals were used to this sort of all-hands approach to medicine—Jodie found herself assisting while Seb did as swift and neat a piece of ocular surgery as she'd seen.

Not that she'd seen much. This was the sort of injury she'd normally send on to Brisbane, and send on fast. Speed was vital here. Even if there was no penetration into the inner eye, foreign bodies moved, they caused infection and the chance of Ruby losing her sight in that eye—or it even causing a sympathetic loss of sight in the other eye—was real.

But because of Seb that risk was minimised. She watched in appreciation of his skill as he mounted a needle on the end of a cotton tip, bending it with sterile forceps. Then, with his hand resting on the sleeping Ruby's cheek, using only the very tips of his long fingers, holding the blade tangentially to the eye surface, he deftly lifted the offending sliver up and away.

The sight of that tiny sliver was such a relief... What a gift, she thought as he irrigated, scrupulously checking and washing out any residual foreign body material, then applying antibiotic ointment and a double eye patch, doubling the inner pad to prevent the eyelid from opening.

'She'll still need to come to Brisbane,' he said. 'I need to repeat fluorescein staining and check vision with the right equipment, but that can wait until tomorrow. As soon as she's awake and the IV's finished, if Cliff can assure us she can be kept quiet for the rest of the day I see no reason why she can't go home now and come across to Brisbane on the ferry tomorrow. A night in hospital might be stressful for the whole family and I think it's avoidable.'

'But it takes weeks—months—to get an appointment with an ophthalmologist,' Jodie said. She knew the drill. Patients who needed urgent care were admitted to hospital. Then the specialist could see them on their morning or evening rounds. It was much more efficient—for the specialist. She also knew ophthalmologists' fee structure. She thought again of Arthur's description of this man as a waste of space—and thought of the doctors whose career plans seemed to be making as much money as possible.

Today this man could be surfing or making money. Donating this morning to his uncle—and now Ruby—must be some sacrifice.

But it seemed he'd made the decision to be generous.

'I'll make time for Ruby,' he told her. 'I'll take details and have my receptionist ring Cliff first thing tomorrow. She'll organise a time after the ferry gets in.'

'That's…kind.'

'Not as kind as saving my uncle.' He smiled again, but this time his smile was rueful. 'Though what you did was kindness to my uncle, not to me. The old man gives me such grief…'

His smile died, but then he gave a decisive nod—moving on? 'Right, then. You agree? I'll go talk to Cliff. As soon as Ruby's drip's through and she's nicely awake we'll all let you sleep.'

'Thank you,' she managed.

And then he frowned. 'Will you sleep?'

'I guess. As long as nothing else happens.' She caught herself then, aware there was a note of pathos in her voice, and he must have heard it. What was she doing, feeling sorry for herself? 'It shouldn't though,' she told him. 'It's a small island. I'll be back surfing in no time.'

'Because that's the way you like it?'

'Absolutely.'

'But he was still watching her, still frowning. 'So no other commitments? You don't have six kids and two dogs waiting at home for Sunday lunch?'

'Heaven forbid,' she said, trying to lighten her voice. 'I don't even have a goldfish, and Angus and Misty—the island's other two doctors—will be back this afternoon so I can go back to being a part-time doctor.'

'You love surfing more than medicine?' He was watching too closely for her liking. What was with the inquisition?

'You like surfing too,' she said, a bit too tartly. 'And your uncle says you don't do family. I suspect we're birds of a feather.'

'And I suspect that we're not,' he said, and his voice was grim again. 'But moving on…let's go see if Cliff has managed to annoy Arthur yet. It doesn't take much to annoy him. He's done more than annoy you, though, so I suspect the sooner we're gone the better you'll like it.'

Which was very true, she conceded, but as he gave her a rueful smile and headed out to deal with his great-uncle…why was she feeling an inexplicable sense of loss?

CHAPTER FOUR

Five months later

'MARRIAGE! YOU HAVE to be kidding.'

This morning Arthur Cantrell had been buried. Given his way, Seb would have organised a small private ceremony but, as per Arthur's pre-paid instructions, a very expensive funeral consortium had conducted an over-the-top ceremony that would have done any of the politicians who'd attended proud.

And there had been politicians. And company directors. And pretty much the entire who's who of Australia's financial world. They'd arrived for the ceremony, shaken Seb's hand—there were no other family hands to shake—and then departed with all possible speed.

None had had any personal affection for Arthur, and at his age his sudden death from a catastrophic heart event had surprised no one. The attending suits had had only one thing in common—they wanted to know who'd now be controlling the massive Cantrell Holdings.

Which could be him. Cue incredulity. Given the animosity between himself and his uncle, he'd never thought of such a possibility.

But now...

He was currently facing a trio of lawyers. With a fortune like this at stake, they'd obviously decided that giving this news was too much responsibility for one man. The law firm's senior partner had just read out his uncle's will, and it had left him stunned.

'Choice?' he managed, struggling to get the word out.

'His original will was firm,' the senior lawyer told him, looking grave. 'But after your great-uncle had that incident on Kirra Island he decided to add a second option.' He shot Seb a nervous glance. 'We have no idea who this Dr Tavish is, but she must have made an impression on him. Given the gravity of the situation, and it is in a sense a bequest to her, we decided to inform her at once. A registered letter should be with her now.'

'But this is ludicrous.'

'We did query the legality as soon as we were made aware of it,' the junior of the trio told him, sounding apologetic. 'Your uncle was elderly, and he'd had major health issues. With such a clause we initially thought that the current board of Cantrell Holdings might be able to argue mental impairment. But your uncle made sure this was watertight. It seems he arranged a consultation with one of Brisbane's top neurologists, and there's now an attached specialist opinion stating he was in sound mind. We don't believe it can be fought.'

'Ludicrous,' he said. Seb had picked up the document and was staring at it as if it might explode.

'Nevertheless, it's what your uncle decreed. You might need time to think about it—maybe consult your own lawyer or lawyers? The current directors of Cantrell certainly will.' The man's severe face twisted into the trace of a bemused smile. 'Is this… Jodie Tavish…someone you might like to marry?'

'You have to be kidding!' For heaven's sake… The thought of marriage, to a woman he'd met once…this was indeed ridiculous. Even marriage itself… There'd never been time in his world and maybe there never would be time. Plus, he hardly remembered her.

But…he did remember her. He fought for images now and found them—Dr Jodie Tavish, battle-worn after a dreadful day and night, injured, weary, but strong. A formidable woman.

But…*marriage*?

'Is she someone you'd object to marrying?' the lawyer was asking. 'The inducements seem… favourable.'

'Favourable? That's surely a joke.'

'I'm afraid it's not a joke.' The senior lawyer was already starting to put papers back in his briefcase. 'As my colleague said, you might like to consult your own lawyers, but the choice seems stark. It's up to you—and this Dr Tavish—to decide.'

* * *

It was eleven in the morning and she was off-duty. Misty was doing clinic. Angus was on duty for house calls or emergencies. Jodie had just had a truly excellent surf, she was now free for the rest of the day, and the day was glorious. She came home, showered and then wandered along the beach path into town for coffee—and maybe a croissant?

Or two croissants, she conceded. Surfing made a woman hungry. She collected her mail, swapped island gossip with the postmistress—Dot—then headed to the baker's. There she bought coffee, a croissant *and* a raspberry Danish, and then settled on the trunk of a palm that had crashed during the storm. Most of the debris had been cleared, but this tree trunk had been left as a lovely place for a seat overlooking the bay. Perfect.

Or almost perfect. There was one thing now marring her contentment—the registered letter Dot had just handed her.

For years, every such official envelope had her thinking: was this Hali trying to reach her? Was it information about her daughter? But she'd had enough let-downs over the years to realise no such information would be forthcoming. Whatever she'd signed, or her parents had signed on her behalf, all those years ago, the stipulation of no contact was pretty much binding.

So now… This'd be something to do with her apartment, she told herself, putting the letter aside until she'd coped with her messy pastry. She still owned her small apartment in Melbourne, and occasionally there were things to deal with on it.

So she finished her first pastry, licked her fingers, turned her attention to her coffee and finally opened the letter.

What the...?

Her coffee splashed over the top of the letter. She stood up, shaking coffee off the thick parchment, ignoring the coffee on her shorts, trying to see the words under the coffee stains.

It wasn't about Hali. Or her apartment. This was absurd.

It was a legal notice from a firm called Noah, Bartram and...and coffee splodge? The paper was thick and creamy, expensive. Even under coffee, it looked very, very formal.

Dear Dr Tavish.
We regret to inform you of the death of our client, Mr Arthur George Cantrell.

Her eyes were blurring—or was that coffee? This wasn't making sense.

...the bequest is as follows. The sum of one million dollars to Dr Jodie Catherine Tavish, on absolute condition that she marry my great-nephew, Dr Sebastian Michael Cantrell.

This marriage must take place within one calendar year of my death, and the marriage must be seen to be genuine, using the rulings for visa requirements for entry of foreign nationals as potential Australian citizens as minimum requirement.

Dr Tavish is also required to sign an agreement setting up a trust fund for any future offspring of this marriage, facilitating the Cantrell name continuing and giving such offspring a controlling interest in the corporation known collectively as Cantrell Holdings...

Ouch! The spilled coffee had scalded her knee and she hadn't even noticed. She noticed now and left letter, remaining coffee and remaining croissant on the bench while she headed for a nearby tap. When she got back the seagulls had pinched her pastry and knocked over her remaining coffee. She watched the croissant being held aloft by no less than three warring seagulls. It was dropped, swooped on by others before it hit the ground and then carried triumphantly out to sea.

'Ridiculous,' she said out loud, staring at the disappearing croissant—and then she looked again at the coffee-stained letter and she even grinned.

She'd had proposals before—of course she had. Almost every young—or youngish—health professional she'd ever met had learned to cope with patients who saw professional caring as something more. Even on the island, one of the old fishermen she'd cared for after a stroke had tried to set her up with his bachelor son. The fact that his son was well over sixty, had a major drinking problem and smelled of fish was irrelevant. 'He's got a great boat,' his dad had told Jodie. 'And so what if he's older than you? That means you have every chance of eventually inheriting his boat.'

This was the same thing, she thought. She'd treated Arthur for what, less than twenty-four hours, and she'd met his great-nephew once. And she didn't even know if his great-nephew normally smelled of fish.

She had looked him up though. She'd had an impressive professional letter from him after he'd followed up with Ruby. She'd been impressed with his skills, and had thought maybe she could continue referring patients to him.

As if. It seemed he was a part-time doctor. A phone call to the Brisbane hospital where he worked had told her he was only there three days a week. He did weekend call work but only for inpatients, and he was booked out months ahead. 'He only takes patients referred within the hospital system,' his receptionist had told her apologetically. 'He has other interests.'

Like surfing?

That'd have to mean he probably didn't smell like fish, she conceded, and a million dollars was probably a better inducement than an ancient fishing boat. But…

'Ridiculous,' she said aloud, and headed back into the post office to buy a postcard and borrow a pen. She might as well get this out of the way fast.

She made her reply formal.

I am in receipt of your letter informing me of the conditional bequest from the estate of Mr Arthur Cantrell. Please take this letter as my definite refusal of such a bequest. Could you also please inform Dr Sebastian Cantrell that my acceptance of this offer is out of the question.

Enough? The letter she'd received appeared to be a valid legal document, so she signed her reply with care, printed her name underneath and asked Dot to co-sign. Then she paid extra for registered post, handed it over to Dot and went to buy another coffee. And, feeling firm, another croissant.

CHAPTER FIVE

HE ARRIVED TWO weeks later. Jodie had just finished work—she was on clinic duty this week but by three she was done. Time for a surf? She walked along the beach track home, rounded the last bend and Dr Seb Cantrell was standing on her front porch.

He looked out of place on her saggy little veranda, with the sea a backdrop that defined her cottage as more of a beach shack. He was dressed casually in chinos and an open-neck shirt, but he didn't look like any of the tourists who frequented the island. Even in casual gear he looked...professional. Like he was here to work?

'Dr Tavish?'

He was wary?

Her wariness went off the charts.

'Dr Cantrell,' she said and waited for more, but he said nothing. What was he doing here?

'I got the lawyer's letter,' she said at last. 'I assume they received my reply. I also assume your great-uncle must have been...'

'Not of sound mind?'

The wariness was still there, and by now she'd assessed him further. He looked exhausted, and maybe even more lean than he'd looked the last time she'd seen him. There were deep lines around his eyes. Strained to breaking point?

Had he been fond of Arthur?

'I'm sorry for your loss,' she said, gently, deciding sympathy was the way to go. 'Was it sudden?'

'In his sleep.' His reply sounded grim. 'It was the way he'd have chosen, though too soon for his liking. He'd have liked to be pulling the strings for another decade or six.'

'I'm sorry,' she said again, and that was followed by more silence.

A flock of lorikeets were arguing with gusto in the eucalypts behind her cottage. Their squawking seemed unreal.

Actually, this whole situation seemed unreal. Why was he here? Had her simple refusal caused complications?

And, finally, he spoke. 'Dr Tavish, seriously, I think I need to marry you.'

And there was a conversation-stopper. Was he kidding? She fingered the phone in her pocket. Maybe she should put in an urgent call to Misty and Angus. *Guys, come fast, bring sedatives and a straitjacket. I suspect hallucinogenic drugs are involved.*

'Well, that's not going to happen,' she said, deciding to be brisk. Professionalism was surely the way to go here. 'I made that clear in my letter. Sorry, Dr Cantrell, but I'm not for sale. Now, if you'll excuse me...'

'Not even for a million?'

She had to walk past him to get into her cottage. This was annoying. Maybe she could remember something she needed at the shops? Excuse herself?

Run?

'Not even for a million,' she told him. 'This is ludicrous.'

'I know, that's how it seems and I'm sorry.' He raked his hair, a gesture she found she remembered, and his look of weariness intensified. 'Maybe I'd better explain.'

There was no way such a proposition could be explained, but the exhaustion on his face had her hesitating. The doctor part of her even had her concerned. Okay, she could give him five minutes.

'Fine,' she told him. 'But I'm not inviting you inside. We stay here on the porch.' There were a couple of families on the beach below the cottage. If she yelled hard enough, she'd get help.

But he didn't seem like the kind of guy who needed a straitjacket, she conceded. He looked...

Suddenly, she wasn't sure how he looked because, weirdly, her body seemed to be remembering that twinge of...something...she'd felt when he'd held her shoulders. What? She didn't have a clue—*and it wasn't wanted now.*

'Are you okay?' she managed, forcing the professional side of her to kick in. The tiredness she was hearing in his voice seemed to be almost bone-deep. She'd seen this before in patients who'd lost someone they loved with all their hearts. Surely, he couldn't have felt this about his uncle. 'You look like you haven't slept for weeks.'

'I'm okay.' He managed a tired smile. 'I'm just between a rock and a hard place.'

'So explain,' she told him, coming to the decision that she might as well put this on a clinical basis. He was clearly in trouble and she was starting to think…irrationality caused by depression?

Where was a psychiatrist when she needed one? There wasn't one on this island. Was she all he had?

'Okay, sit,' she told him, and she got a look that said, astonishingly, that he got it. A tired smile lit his eyes.

'You're going to charge for a consultation?'

'You can give my receptionist your billing details later,' she told him. 'You want me to get you a box of tissues before we start?'

'It's not that bad.'

'Your eyes say it is,' she said gently, continuing in the way she'd decided to play it. 'So sit down and tell me.'

So he sat on one of her old porch chairs and, despite his refusal, she fetched a tissue box and sat it firmly on the rickety table in front of him. His smile emerged again as he saw it. 'As if,' he said.

'Neglecting to place tissues in reach of adult

males would be an omission that's both sexist and ageist,' she told him as she sat herself. 'Deal with it.'

'I promise there won't be tears. It's not that bad. Or, rather, it is but I won't…'

'Don't promise anything. Just tell me.'

He cast her a curious look. 'You sound like a professional.'

'That's because I am, though I would have thought you'd have done a serious background check before proposing.'

'It's my great-uncle who's proposing—' he winced '—or commanding.'

'And I'm trying hard not to laugh at the proposal and pack you back on the ferry with instructions to the crew to keep you confined,' she said bluntly.

His smile emerged again—and, stupidly, the smile made her feel less than professional—but her growing conviction that here was a man exhausted to the point of collapse grew.

'Explain,' she said again. 'This is to do with your great-uncle's will, right?'

'Of course it is. I assume…' He raked his hair again. 'The thought of a million dollars wouldn't…'

'Please don't go there. The idea of buying me as a bride is nonsense. Leave me out of the equation for a moment. Tell me why you haven't slept.'

Once again, she got a look that said she'd surprised him. He sat for a while longer and she decided to think of the surf forecast, and the fact that her front garden needed weeding, or that she'd forgotten to buy anything for dinner tonight. Anything. Her personal mantra, set in stone fifteen years back, was not to feel emotion. Not to get involved.

But then…why was the look on this man's face making her feel distress?

'You know my great-uncle is…*was* head of Cantrell Holdings,' he said at last and she hauled her attention away from the possibility of takeaway pizza and decided to focus. She'd just told him she was a professional, she told herself. She knew how to keep boundaries in place. Sort of.

'Yes,' she said briefly.

'And you know how big Cantrell is?'

'Huge,' she agreed. She had done a little investigation after Arthur had left, and realised she had heard of it. 'Aren't there big environmental issues though? Mining on the reef, damage from leaching from mines, that sort of thing?'

'There are massive issues,' he agreed. 'But Cantrell has the resources to ride roughshod over any concerns, and the fact that its controlling interests have been privately owned has meant the government has had trouble touching it, or influencing its direction. Now, though, I have the chance to move to the helm of Cantrell.'

'Hooray,' she said, but noncommittally. There was still so much she didn't understand here. 'I assume you're pleased?'

'I'm appalled.' He paused and stared down towards the beach for a while. There were kids playing in the shallows while their mums watched, their squeals drifting up on the warm breeze. The scene looked idyllic. Sebastian's face said this was anything but idyllic.

'Can I explain background?' he said at last.

'You risk taking this from a short to long consultation,' she told him. 'That'll cost you thirty dollars extra.'

'I'll risk it,' he said with another tired smile and then forged on.

'My whole family is wealthy,' he told her. 'But not always. My great-grandfather was born on a farm in outback Queensland but hated farming. He moved away to do engineering. When his father died, he returned—reluctantly—to the farm, and at a time when drought was forcing a lot of farmers off the land, he found high grade coal. He persuaded a couple of friends to help him buy the surrounding land, he quietly bought up mining licenses, then approached small mining companies and offered to share profits. Within a couple of years, he was able to buy his friends out, take control of the mining himself and the rest is history.'

'And the Cantrells have been mining ever since?'

'Not my side of the family,' he said wearily. 'My great-grandfather had two children, sons, Arthur—my great-uncle—and Frank, my grandfather. Frank died just after my father was born, and Arthur never married, so Arthur's been pretty much in control of the company ever since.'

'I'm not seeing…'

'I'm getting there.' He flashed her a look of annoyance—she was obviously interrupting a story he wanted to get over with fast. 'Sorry. I hate this. Anyway, the long and short of it is that when my grandfather died my father ended up owning half the company, but he hated it and sold it to Arthur. Arthur objected—violently—but my father gave him no choice. He did medicine—ophthalmology, like me. He met my mother, another eye specialist, and together they used the funds they'd received from the sale to set up a foundation to provide critical eyecare in Al Delebe.'

The sudden switch had her blinking. 'Al Delebe?'

'You won't have heard of it. Hardly anyone has. It's a tiny African nation wedged between two bigger and much more warlike ones. It's so small and war-torn that few aid agencies are on the ground. Mum and Dad were intrepid travellers. They went there on their honeymoon, but instead of sightseeing they found themselves treating eyes. That care's been ongoing and it's so important. The heat and dust, the poverty, the lack of education… Jodie, for less than most of us pay for a basic meal, we can remove cataracts, restore someone's sight. For a few lessons teaching basic eyecare, we can save kids from glaucoma, from sight-threatening infections, from a lifetime of blindness.'

Whoa. This conversation was getting away from her. She was staring at him in astonishment, hearing the passion in his voice but totally confounded as to where this was heading.

'So?' she said cautiously.

'So,' he repeated, heavily now. 'I now have a choice. My parents' funds have pretty much been spent—setting up a hospital and attracting staff has bitten into what was a massive fortune. They worked for peanuts, but most doctors won't. Within a couple of years, the funding will run out.'

'Are your parents still involved?'

'They were, until they were killed in a border skirmish twelve years ago.'

That made her flinch. 'I'm sorry.'

'Don't be,' he said, though the brusqueness in his voice told her there was still pain. 'They loved the country; they loved what they were doing and they knew the risks. I'm just sorry they didn't have more time.'

'And you?' The situation now had her intrigued.

'I worked there for a while,' he told her. 'Now I run operations from Brisbane.'

Really? She eyed the tissue box with distrust. This wasn't turning out to be the empathic mental health consultation she'd planned.

'So…um…me?' she ventured at last. 'A million dollars. Marriage. I'm not seeing the connection.'

'If you don't marry me, the foundation will fail.'

She stared at him open-mouthed, and then carefully raised her hand and pushed her mouth closed. 'Huh?' she managed. Okay, that wasn't the most intelligent of responses, but it was all she could get out.

He was looking at her now with something that seemed…a lot like sympathy? As if he knew she wouldn't want to hear this messy story.

'For years, Arthur hated that my father insisted on leaving the business,' he told her. 'To be frank, he was gutted when his brother—my grandfather—died. For him, the company was his only remaining family, and my father refusing to be part of it seemed like deciding to chop off part of him. Dad's decision to take his inheritance rather than invest it into more and more mines—well, to Arthur that was yet another gut-wrench. We were all that was left of his family. He couldn't understand us, he was grief-stricken—and his response was to put every waking minute of his life into building the company.'

'But…this doesn't fit,' she said slowly. 'The Arthur I knew… Every waking minute… How does that fit with deciding to surf when he was over eighty?'

'That was me,' he said heavily. 'We had a huge row just before he came over to the island. He knew the foundation was running out of money, that it couldn't continue for much longer, and he was pressuring me again to return to the company. He accused me of never thinking of anything but my "do-gooding", as he called it. And I countered that he never thought of anything but how much money he could make out of destroying the planet. I was also worried about his health. He was demanding I spend time with him, learning about the company. He held out the carrot that if I did, he might be persuaded to do something for us—and in desperation I said if he did something outside his office I'd think about it. He had major health issues—he had so little time left to enjoy. To be honest, I never dreamed he'd do it. But he obviously planned to take one weekend away and then come back and throw it in my face.'

'Ouch.'

'As you say. And now I'm dealing with his will.'

'Which is?' She was intrigued, but there were major warnings blaring in her head. Back away! This was surely none of her business.

But she'd asked and now he was forging ahead.

'He's given me…us…two options,' he was saying, looking down towards the kids on the beach—carefully not looking at her? 'And they depend on what I do. Or… I'm sorry, but in part it's what you do. The first is that I do nothing. I inherit nothing. The directors will stay as they are, and profits, plus his personal fortune, will continue to be funnelled into further coal mining, plus huge gas exploration off the coast. Both of which will cause untold environmental damage. All profits will be distributed to shareholders. Many people are about to become seriously rich.'

'But not you?'

'Not me.' His face was bleak. 'I guess… I had hoped that he'd leave at least part of the company to me. I couldn't have influenced the way it was run but I could have sold my shareholding and used it to keep the Al Delebe foundation going for a few more years. If you knew how many people's sight that would have saved…'

He stopped at that, just stayed silent, staring down at the beach. The sounds of the children playing on the sand had faded. Everything seemed to have faded.

'But there's another option?' she said at last, trying to figure this out. 'Which is where I come in?'

'The marriage option.'

'With me? That's so crazy.'

'I agree. It is crazy, but you need to hear what's behind it.' He hesitated again, but she stayed silent. And finally he spoke slowly, heavily, as if forcing every word out.

'Arthur was obsessed with family,' he said. 'And you have no idea how much he pressured me to join the company. The first draft of his will, leaving everything to shareholders—was obviously made in frustration—he'd given up on me. But then he met you.'

'Which shouldn't have made one whit of difference.'

'Do you think I don't know that?' He spread his hands. 'It's senseless, but he was obviously impressed, really impressed—so impressed that he thought of another way to force my hand. Marriage. Marriage to you.'

She was starting to feel like she was surrounded by snakes. Cautious didn't begin to describe it, but anger was now cutting through caution. She was starting to feel trapped and she didn't like it one bit. 'If that's not ridiculous...'

'From his point of view it wasn't so ridiculous,' he told her. 'I don't know what you talked about that night, but somehow, he decided that you're ideal breeding stock.'

'Breeding stock!'

He managed a smile then, but a crooked one. 'Good child-bearing hips? A nice fertile woman?'

'What...? Thanks very much!'

He grinned, but then he shrugged and the smile died. 'Sorry. I'm only trying to imagine what Arthur saw. To say he was a misogynist would be an understatement—he had no time for women—but you did save his life. Maybe he wanted to reward you and he thought this was a way to do it. And maybe he thought this might just be a last-ditch plan to bring the company back into the family.'

'But it's crazy.'

'Yes, it is,' he said, in that heavy voice again.

'But in hospital, recovering from a fright, with a battered body and a faltering heart, he wrote a second option into his will. He seriously proposed that we marry, and marry…seriously. For it to work we'd need to live together for at least two years, to satisfy the legal eagles that the marriage is real. But if we agree… His plan seemed to be that you get your million dollars, I inherit his personal fortune and we have children.' He put up a hand as if to ward off her instinctive reaction. 'No. Please, just listen. If that happened, the majority shareholding of the company—all his shares—would be put in a family trust—the Cantrell Family Trust—until the kids he suggested we have come of age. The company can't be sold before they come of age, but I believe he decided that, even if I'm obstinate and keep doing my work abroad, by the time any offspring have grown they'll have come to their senses and Cantrells will once again rule the world.'

She stared at him, growing more and more stunned. This was absurd.

'It's crazy,' she said at last, starting to feel like she was a parrot, repeating the word over and over. *Crazy, crazy, crazy.* 'A trust? *Children?*'

'The lawyers seem to think we wouldn't have to have them,' he said weakly. 'For some reason, Arthur thought it might happen if…if he forced us to live together.'

'In your dreams,' she managed. 'In *his* dreams. And you? Where would that leave you?'

'Well, that's the chink in the armour,' he said, deciding to focus on the beach again, carefully not looking at her. 'This last option was put in just after you'd treated him—it was dictated to his secretary while he was still in hospital in Brisbane. He'd obviously been badly frightened. He wanted the change done in a hurry, so he didn't have lawyers help draft it. A nurse co-signed it, and for some reason he forgot to outline who'd control that trust. It's a big omission because, as he's called it the Cantrell Family Trust, the lawyers believe control would come to me.'

'You...'

'So they say. And even if there are no children, it'll remain with me. It seems I can do anything bar sell the company outright, but the corporation itself can now be redirected, beginning to undo all the damage the company's done. And I can channel his personal fortune to Al Delebe. Jodie...'

Enough. The feeling of being trapped was suddenly overwhelming.

'Stop!'

How did she begin to deal with this? She rose and walked down the steps into the garden, then decided to focus on her breathing for a while. For some reason, breathing seemed really hard. She stared out at the sea; she concentrated on getting her heart rate settled—this seemed incredibly important—and then she took a deep breath and returned to the veranda. It wasn't Seb doing the manipulating, she told herself. It was one scheming old man. She might be angry, but maybe this anger shouldn't be directed at Seb.

He, too, was a puppet.

'So,' she said at last, 'how much money are we talking?'

And he told her. She stood stock-still while he outlined the value of Arthur's personal fortune and how much the company was worth. He told her how much good that personal fortune could do to an impoverished people. He told her how the mining company could be redirected to green energy, to repairing environmental damage. He spoke with passion, with commitment, with emotion, and when finally he paused she felt as if she had nothing left in her. She had nowhere to go.

'But…but you,' she said at last, weakly, fighting to find loopholes. 'This isn't…you. You don't even work full-time. You're like me—you don't commit.'

'How do you know that?'

'Your uncle said. And your receptionist. I rang and tried to get an appointment for one of the islanders who's suffering from what I think is a corneal dystrophy. She said you only worked in the mornings, and you won't take on any patients outside the hospital.'

'I work for the foundation.'

'What, in all your spare time?'

'Yes.'

She frowned. 'So why aren't you in Al Delebe if you care so much?'

That brought more silence, this time seemingly loaded. His face seemed to freeze.

'You're assuming…'

'I'm not assuming,' she flashed back at him. 'I'm asking, and if you want me to take this stupid thing seriously then I need answers. It's you who's assuming that I might even consider this. How do you even know I'm free to marry? There's an assumption.'

'I believe Arthur asked his secretary to find out for him. She told me he believed you were aching to marry.'

'He what?' It was practically a screech.

'Okay.' He held up his hands as if in surrender. 'I apologise.'

'I don't need your apologies,' she snapped. 'How dare he?'

'That's pretty much what I think. He was a scheming, manipulative old man, obsessive about one thing, and he's still pulling strings to continue that obsession from the grave.'

'Oh, this is dumb,' she said, suddenly weary of the whole discussion. 'We might as well finish this now. I don't do commitment. I don't do family and I surely don't sell myself. You're telling me you can save the world if I agree? That's not a plan, it's blackmail. And tell me how your life would change if you went ahead with this. Would you go back to Al Delebe? Would you expect me to go with you?'

'I expect we'd stay in Brisbane,' he said tentatively. 'You could still work, though you wouldn't need to. Of course, all your expenses would be met. Your inheritance would be on top of that. Jodie, I haven't thought that far but...'

'But don't bother.' She was trying hard to sound calm, maybe even get this back on some sort of professional footing. 'So let me see. You marry me, you send a lot of cash to this charity, you then control a huge corporation and you go happily on with the lifestyle you have now?'

'I have no choice,' he said, goaded.

'What, no choice but to work part-time in Australia, earning your over-the-top specialist salary rather than giving your expertise to a people you care so much about?'

And the look on his face—the anger... But mixed with the anger she also saw distress.

But how was his face so readable? This was weird. It was almost like there was some link...

There was no link. Nothing about this made sense, but when he spoke again, the anger and the distress were still there. 'I can't go back to Al Delebe,' he said, as if goaded.

'Why not? Is it so unsafe? Your parents...'

'It's not unsafe in that sense, at least not at the moment. But I can't…'

'Why not?'

'It's personal.'

'So's marriage,' she snapped. 'Get over it. I need facts if you even want me to think about this.'

He closed his eyes, and once again she got the impression of someone carrying a load that seemed almost too great to bear. And with that came an inexplicable urge to respond. Not with more speech, more questions, but suddenly her instinct was to walk forward and give comfort. To take his hands and hold?

This was surely crazy. Where was her professional detachment when she needed it? What was it about this man that made her want…?

No. She wanted nothing. Somehow, she managed not to move. It cost an effort, but she waited, and finally he spoke again.

'If you must know…'

'It's your decision to tell me. I'm probably going nowhere with this, but I'm definitely going nowhere without facts.'

His gaze locked on hers. There was a long moment where she saw pain. The urge to walk forward and take his hands grew again, and inexplicably she wanted to withdraw her demand. Withdraw from this whole situation?

She should, but she didn't, and finally he responded.

'I spent a lot of time there when I was a kid, with my parents,' he told her, and his voice was now clipped and harsh. 'I was home schooled but, almost as soon as I remember, Mum and Dad had me working in the wards, doing everything I could. But in my teens I caught dengue fever. I was fourteen and fit. It wasn't a bad dose but it was enough to make my parents super-cautious.'

'Transmitted by mosquitos?'

'Of course. I can't tell you how much insect-repellent I went through, but after that my parents sent me back here. I was in boarding school in Brisbane and my parents only let me go over during the dry season. I spent holidays with school friends here during the wet season. But then, when I was almost through university, my parents were killed in a border incursion. I went back to help repatriate their bodies and I caught it again. But it was okay,' he said quickly, maybe responding to concern on her face. How could she help herself feeling it? 'The second dose is supposed to be severe but I somehow got off lightly.'

She nodded, satisfied that at least this explanation made sense. 'So you can't risk it again?'

'I felt… I had to,' he said, his voice again heavy. 'I had to see their work continue, and as soon as I qualified I was over there. I was an adult, I told myself, and I was so damned careful. I was vaccinated. I took every precaution possible, but eighteen months ago it hit again, haemorrhagic dengue, and it nearly killed me. So that's it. I may be idealistic but I'm not suicidal. Tropical countries are out for me for ever. I work as hard as I can from here. I know I could do more over there but...'

'But you're no use to anyone dead.'

'No.'

As excuses went for not heading back to a country like Al Delebe, this was a no-brainer. A second dose of dengue fever often killed. A third time... he'd been extraordinarily lucky to survive.

No wonder he was hunkering down in Brisbane.

'So when your uncle described you as a waste of space...' she said slowly.

'I don't waste time—I don't have enough time. I organise the administration from over here. I do online tutorials to train our staff—I need to keep my skills up because of that—and I fundraise. I give presentations to every fundraising organisation that'll have me.'

'So days off?'

'There's a reason I'm not married—I simply don't have time for it. If you marry me, you'll hardly see me.'

There was a statement to take her breath away. This was starting to feel like a punch to the stomach. Or serial punches.

'Cut it out,' she managed. 'Enough of marriage.'

'You mean you won't consider it?'

'No!' And then she paused and finally she

said…slowly, almost fearfully, 'You say…you don't have time for marriage. Have you even thought how this could work?'

And she saw a light in his eyes. She held out her hands instinctively, a gesture that might be seen as warding him off, but he didn't move.

'It might,' he told her, suddenly careful and obviously neutral. 'Believe it or not, I have thought this through. It's important enough to consider.'

'So tell me.'

He nodded, took a deep breath and appeared to dive in. Talking a bit too fast. 'It'd have to look real,' he told her. 'We'd need a decent apartment, or a house where we could have our own space, but we'd need…my lawyers tell me…something like a bathroom set up for two, a bedroom that looks like it's shared. No one's going to break in in the middle of the night to check, but we could be given less than a day's notice. And that might happen. The suits currently controlling the company, the minor shareholders, have a lot to lose. The façade of our marriage would have to continue for a couple of years. But we could be independent. I'm so damned busy and you could keep on with your surfing, your part-time medicine, whatever. I imagine that could happen anywhere. But children…' He hesitated and then forged on. 'I… There was a letter included in the will. My uncle said you're hungry for babies.'

It was like a slap. She stood silently, feeling the

colour drain from her face, feeling almost dizzy. *Hungry for babies*, she thought. No.

Hungry for a baby.

For her fifteen-year-old daughter.

'Jodie?' He must have seen her instinctive flinch. She backed away, her hands coming up again.

'No.'

'I'm sorry. Jodie, did I…?'

'Nothing,' she managed. 'Leave it. The last thing I want is babies.'

He was still watching her intently, obviously seeing—well, he couldn't see it, she told herself—a pain that she'd hidden for so long. But obviously he decided to keep going.

'Well, that's a relief, because neither do I,' he said, but he still sounded…puzzled. 'As far as I'm concerned, this would be a business arrangement only, although it'd have to look more from the outside. Maybe we'd need to attend a few fundraisers as a couple, that sort of thing. But Jodie…'

'No buts.' She was starting to feel panic. 'Leave it,' she told him and closed her eyes for a moment, desperately trying to assemble her thoughts. This was a lunatic scheme, not to be thought of, not to be even imagined.

But…

There were buts. She knew it. There was a voice in the back of her head, scrambling to be heard through the panic, that said, *Jodie, honestly, if you calm down then maybe, just maybe, you could do some good here.* Without being involved?

All her life, well, all her life since Hali, she'd fought to stay apart. The pain of that time, the loss of her daughter, her parents' absolute rejection, had scarred her bone-deep, and the fear of letting anyone close had ruled everything she'd done since.

She'd learned to live with it. She'd also managed to put pain aside and have a fun life. She'd made good friends—okay, superficially, but people who were fun to be with. She'd enjoyed her medical training and that was useful and satisfying. She taught surfing now, and that was fun and useful. Her life was pretty much how she liked it.

But the voice in the back of her head was now starting to insist.

If this guy is really serious...if what he says is true...maybe my actions could make a difference to so many people. Maybe I could do some real good.

And at little cost to herself.

She could still hold herself apart—in fact, that was what he seemed to be asking. There were technicalities that'd have to be ironed out—lots of technicalities. Some sort of contract, she thought, a document known to exist only by the two of them.

She'd have to trust.

There was a biggie. She met his gaze and he looked back at her. He was silent, maybe seeing that this was the moment where everything hung in the balance.

Did she believe him? Was this a real thing? It seemed preposterous and yet, looking at him, she was seeing trouble in his eyes, seeing need…

But she was also seeing concern. He was worried about her?

Well, that was crazy. To him, she'd only be a means to an end. If they were to continue down this crazy path, he'd have to be that to her.

And yet…

All her life she'd held back. There'd been dates in the past, flings, fun forays into the world of romance.

Or not really romance because she was only ever in it for a good time, and she'd always made that clear. So…could she do it again? Could she do it for this?

'We *would* be separate,' he told her, and it was as if he was reading her mind.

'Two years…'

'That's what my lawyers say. Jodie, you could consider it a job offer, and a good one. There're not many jobs that come with a million-dollar bonus paid upfront.'

'I don't care about your money.'

But did she? There were things she could do…

'But will you think about it?' His voice was gentle now, as if sensing she was wavering.

Oh, this was nuts. She was feeling dizzy, as if

she was in the middle of some twisted dream and needed to wake up.

But Seb's voice said this was no dream. His gaze said this was deadly serious, and so much was at stake.

'I need facts,' she said, a trifle desperately. 'All the facts. And I need time. I want everything you can throw at me about the foundation, facts from inside and out. I want facts about Cantrell Holdings and I want facts about you. Leave nothing out, and I mean nothing. I need time to gain an independent view.'

'We have a month,' he said cautiously. 'And I'd need to know about you as well.'

'What you see is what you get,' she said bluntly. 'But you probably won't get. Give me two weeks, Seb, and then we'll talk about this again.'

'You mean you will consider it?'

'I… Maybe.'

'There's no one else?' he asked cautiously. 'No partner? No…'

'No,' she snapped. 'Not that it's any of your business.' And then she couldn't help herself. 'You?'

'I've never had time for dating.'

'You're kidding. Are you as obsessed as your uncle?'

'I care about what I do,' he said neutrally. 'Jodie, the million dollars…'

'Will you shut up about the money?'

'It's all about the money.'

'If it was then I'd say leave now,' she snapped. 'But if my research says this might well change people's lives… Well, you implied that a gun was being held to your head. Maybe this is a gun being held to mine.'

'That's nonsensical.' He paused and then said seriously, 'Okay. Jodie, I know this is crazy but the gun isn't being pointed at either of us. It's being pointed at the eyesight of so many of the most vulnerable people in the world.'

'That has to be an overstatement.'

'I'll send you the facts,' he told her. 'All I ask is that you consider them with an open mind.'

He left soon after, catching the ferry back to Brisbane. He'd brought work to do on the boat, but in the end he didn't open his satchel. Instead, he let his mind drift over what had just happened.

In the two weeks since he'd read the will, he'd had time to investigate. What he'd learned was that Jodie Tavish was bright, exceedingly well qualified and out for a good time.

Her university record spoke of brilliance—it seemed she could have gone into any specialty she'd wanted. But instead of more lucrative career paths, she'd gone down the route of family medicine, committing herself to train with some of the best doctors in the field. Her reports from that time were impeccable.

Most doctors though, after that intense training, would have devoted themselves to their career. Family medicine was usually the specialty of those who liked personal involvement, who valued getting to know patients for the long term, treating everyday illnesses but also being there for the birth-to-death dramas that eventually encompassed all.

But not Jodie. From the time she'd finished training she'd moved from job to job, working as a locum, a fill-in for doctors wanting a break, for communities that were temporarily short-staffed. She'd pretty much made a career of it. The only constant in her career choice seemed to be the need to be close to the surf.

His mind had pretty much closed against her when he'd realised that. A doctor who put surfing first.

This last job though, the first time she seemed to have put down roots, was the position on Kirra Island. She'd been there for over two years so maybe she was starting to get involved. He'd been impressed by her actions when Arthur had been injured, and a careful phone call to a colleague he knew on the medical board had confirmed that impression.

'Jodie Tavish? Kirra Island? There's a great medical set-up—I wish we could have that sort of arrangement in all our remote communities. They're three excellent doctors giving an excellent service. Misty's been there long-term—I gather it was her family home. She was overloaded for years until finally she married Angus and they split the load. Then they persuaded Jodie to work there as well. On the surface they look like they treat their careers as a holiday job, but every one of them puts intense effort into keeping their skills current. You know the point system we have each year to make sure our people are up-to-date? The points those three accrue would just about cover every medical practice south of Brisbane. If Jodie's treating your uncle… Well, to answer your question, our only beef is that we could use her full-time in so many other places, but in our view there's no finer doctor.'

So there was no quibble about her skills. It was only her personality.

Her desire to surf when she should be working?

And then he thought…was the word *should* appropriate?

What was there in his head that made him think what she was doing was a cop-out?

He sat on the front deck of the ferry and let his thoughts drift. There were a couple of dolphins surfing on the bow wave of the ferry, enjoying themselves.

'Shouldn't you guys be fishing?' he said, almost to himself, and realised that was exactly what he was thinking about Jodie. What was she doing, wasting her time, when she could be committing…?

She'd made it very clear that she didn't commit. But he wasn't asking her to commit, he told himself. She could continue playing and working as she was doing now. She could spend a couple of years sharing a house with him. She'd have a million dollars in the bank for herself while she lived off the Cantrell profits. Maybe she could cut back on medicine, surf even more?

That was what he'd thought when he'd had time to consider his uncle's preposterous will. It was why he'd decided to try and argue his case today. Jodie was a part-time doctor to whom surfing seemed paramount. She could marry him and keep surfing. If she wanted, she could get another part-time job in Brisbane but there'd be no need. She could live entirely at his expense for two years and her life wouldn't need to change at all.

So, what was there in today's meeting that told him it wouldn't be that easy?

The dolphins surfed on, but as they neared the mainland they veered off—finally to pay attention to their dinner? And Seb's attention was caught by a group of kids on the shoreline, dressed in some sort of scouting uniform, sweeping the shore for litter.

'Yeah, that's reality,' he told himself. 'Some of us need to work to help the world. Surely Jodie will see…'

But then he let himself think of Jodie as he'd last seen her, standing confused in the sunlight, looking at him with a gaze that saw...more than he wanted her to see?

He'd thought this proposition might be simple, but now...

There were depths he couldn't see, he conceded. Things his background check couldn't reveal.

What was in her head? What was driving her?

It couldn't matter. All he knew was that it was imperative she marry him, that she lived with him for two years as his wife.

His wife.

She was beautiful.

Why was he thinking that?

And it wasn't true, he told himself, or not...not beautiful in what was maybe the world's view of what a gorgeous woman *should* look like.

She was tall, almost as tall as he was, and he was six feet. She wasn't thin like the world of fashion seemed to decree was desirable. Her body looked lithe, fit and muscled. Today she'd been wearing scuffed sandals and he'd noticed sand between her toes—sand after a day doing clinical work? It was almost as if the sand was part of who she was. And her hair was...gorgeous?

But then he thought...no, not gorgeous. It was long, blonde and tangled, as if a comb had been pulled through in a hurry but the tangles had been left as too much to bother with. She had freckles under her wide blue eyes, and the lips on her generous mouth seemed permanently twitched upward—as if her permanent state was laughter.

Okay, he conceded. She was beautiful.

How would he feel being married to such a woman?

No. Not married, he told himself. Marriage had never been on his agenda.

He had thought about it, though—of course he had—but he'd deliberately thought *no*. If he ever married it would need to be to someone as passionate about his work as he was, who wouldn't demand that he back off from the forces that drove him. It'd need to be a marriage such as his parents had, where work was everything.

And the thought of his parents' marriage… where work was everything…where their only child had felt himself an outsider, someone to fit around the edges of their shared passion…it left him cold.

But he'd just proposed to Jodie. If they lived together for two years…if Arthur was right and she did indeed want children…

She'd shrugged off the idea as laughable and that was just as well, he thought. Children…

A wife…

Not a wife, he told himself harshly. He'd be house sharing and he'd be acting, nothing more. And with so much at stake, maybe he could do it.

Maybe it wouldn't mess with his life. It wasn't as if he'd have free time to spend sharing.

Sharing Jodie's life.

What was she thinking now?

They were pulling up at the dock. As he headed for the gangplank, he thought he'd done all he could.

He'd asked a woman to marry him. He'd asked Jodie to save lives. He could only hope that the indecision, the concern he'd seen flash through those deep blue eyes meant that she cared.

But part of him was already thinking...if she cared...

For him?

Yeah, right. Shove that thought right out of your mind, he told himself. It was only if she didn't care, if neither of them cared, that this thing could possibly work.

CHAPTER SIX

HE WAS WHO he said he was.

In the hours and days after Seb left, her online searches seemed to spit out information almost faster than she could take it in. There were links to videos of field hospitals in Al Delebe, to online tutorials run by Seb, to fundraising events, to discussion and assessment of his charity in reputable broadsheets and so much more.

It seemed this whole proposal was genuine.

The older online tutorials, those aimed at staff on the ground, were the most illuminating. She approached them with a certain amount of distrust, but soon she felt astounded. She was watching Seb at work in Al Delebe.

She saw a training video following a little girl, surely not more than six, born with congenital cataracts, almost blind from birth. She saw Seb's initial consultation and examination, the reasons for surgery being carefully outlined. Then, in what looked like a field hospital, in a makeshift operating theatre, she saw the child being comforted by her parents until the anaesthetic took effect. She saw Seb's reassurance, both to the child and to her parents, and to her astonishment Seb was speaking seamlessly in their own language. The video was dubbed in English, but even if it wasn't she could see the trust the family had in him.

She watched on as the little girl slipped into sedation, as the well-trained medical team took over. Led by Seb.

The procedure was complex—this was surely something that needed to be done in a major teaching hospital, but there was no doubting his skill. As he worked, he spoke out loud for the camera's sake, or maybe for the sake of a cluster of trainees in the background. He was explaining what he was doing every step of the way.

When he asked for anything, from the senior nurse, from the anaesthetist, even from the elderly man who stood in the background, seemingly as a gofer—he explained what he was asking for, directing whoever was behind the camera to pan to illustrate. And all this time his focus was absolutely on what he was doing.

Finally, as the little girl was wheeled out of the theatre, she saw him turn to the trainees and talk them through what he'd done. He also talked of amblyopia—the problems associated with the child's vision having been restricted from birth— and suggestions as to follow-up advice.

And then she saw the final consultation, a little girl awed and her parents unbelieving—their little girl could see.

This video alone left her feeling winded, humbled by the depth of his skills. She checked the stats online and saw this one clip had been watched so many times it made her head spin. Who by? Surely not just those in Al Delebe. Even though it was in the local language, the subtitles meant this could be a teaching tool the world over.

She also found news clips, incidents where neighbouring fighting had spilled into the country. She saw pictures of Seb, hauled out of his world of saving sight to save bomb victims, to be there for the casualties of war.

She thought of the words Arthur had used to describe his great-nephew.

'He's a waste of space...'

As if. He was driven, she thought. Driven as his uncle had been, but for such a cause...

So, finally, she let herself think seriously of what he was proposing—what he had proposed. Surely it had to be ridiculous, but the more she watched, the more a voice in her head was starting to say... *This isn't about me. It's about so much more.*

The thought was almost overwhelming. She desperately wanted to back away, but somehow, she made herself work on, doing her own research as well as following the links Seb had sent her. She worked through reams of information about the Cantrell mines, about the power the company held, about their reputation for riding roughshod over anything and anyone who got in the way of profits.

The voice was growing louder.

But…*marriage*?

Finally, she reached the point where she had to talk to someone—someone who wasn't Seb. So, a week later, she ended up sitting in Misty and Angus's kitchen, spilling everything to her friend and colleague.

This big and messy house had always seemed a haven for Jodie. Angus was out for the evening—island choir, for heaven's sake—and it seemed Misty's grandma was at bingo. Their two kids were asleep. Jodie was on call for any medical need, but the island seemed quiet and the decision she was about to make was doing her head in.

So she set her laptop on the kitchen table, loaded the video of Seb's tutorial and asked Misty to watch it. Then she showed her the website of Cantrell Holdings.

A bemused Misty watched—and then listened incredulously as she outlined Seb's proposal.

To say Misty was thunderstruck would have been an understatement. She stared without saying a word for what surely must have been three or four minutes. 'We need wine,' she managed at last. 'How dare you tell me this when I'm pregnant and you're on call?'

'I'm dizzy already and wine might make me even dizzier,' Jodie told her. 'Best not.'

'So…so what are you going to do?'

'Marry him?' Jodie managed. 'I think I have to.'

'Marry!' Her friend was staring at her as if she was out of her mind. 'This is like something out of fantasy fiction, it can't possibly be real.'

But then she looked again at the image of Seb on the foundation's website—they both looked— and Misty frowned in concentration. 'I've heard of this foundation. What they're doing is stunning. Jodie, the difference...'

'I know.' It was practically a moan.

'And he looks nice too,' Misty said, still sounding dazed. 'In the video...spunky?'

'Spunky?'

'I'm looking at the overall picture here,' her friend said hastily. 'You have to admit he looks hot.'

'Misty...'

'Yeah, not a factor,' Misty agreed, somehow hauling herself together. 'Or...it shouldn't be. But it's not like you're being asked to marry the great-uncle.'

'But...marriage?'

'I know,' Misty said, sounding dazed again, but then she appeared to think it through. 'But it's only for two years. And I've read about arranged marriages. If you take romance out of the equation, you might even be able to make it work. As long as you're emotionally and physically safe, as long as you have and give respect, and as long as you like being in their company, the chances for a decent marriage are predicted to be pretty good.'

'That sounds…clinical.'

'Maybe, but we're talking a house share situation for two years.' She gazed again at the screen. 'I don't know. What do you have to lose?'

'So much.' She closed her eyes.

'This island?' Misty asked, her voice gentling. 'Your work here? We could cope without you.'

'But you're about to have a baby. You'll need time off and that'd mean only one doctor on the island.'

'We'll cope,' Misty said stolidly. 'For something like this… Think of what else is at stake.' And then her voice softened. 'Jodie, what else is scaring you?'

'Him,' she said, before she could stop herself.

'Seb?' Misty looked again at the image on the screen, the front page of the foundation's website. It was a plea for funds, so the image tried to evoke emotion. On the screen was a photograph of Seb, stooping to talk to a young mother. She was holding her little boy in her arms, the child had a patch over one eye and the hope and trust on both their faces was almost tangible.

The gentleness and professional reassurance on Seb's seemed equally real.

'He looks wonderful,' Misty said. 'Is there

something I'm not getting? Jodie, would you be afraid to marry him?'

'No. I… Yes.'

'Because?'

'Because I don't want to be… I don't want to be…'

'Drawn into caring?' Misty ventured. 'I get that.' She hesitated. 'Jodie, this is way beyond my ability—or right—to even think about giving advice. I know you've always held yourself apart. Sometimes I've even tried to guess why, but I won't ask. It's none of my business. Bottom line is that this has to be your decision and your decision alone. If you can't do this then there'll be no judgement from me. We'll forget this whole conversation.'

And then, blessedly, Jodie's phone rang. She answered and rose, with some relief. 'Croup,' she said, and Misty nodded.

'You know you're needed here,' she said softly. 'And you're doing good. We all do what we can. Go and deal with croup, Jodie love.' And then she gave her friend an impulsive hug. 'There's no judgement from anyone if you can't do more. But…'

'But?'

'But, no pressure, love, but if everything else fits…he does look really, really sexy.'

'That can't possibly fit into the equation.'

'I don't see why not!' Misty retorted with a grin. 'There's no rule about life not being fun.'

The call from Jodie a week later was brusque, to say the least.

'We need to talk. Can you come this afternoon? I'll meet you at the ferry.'

Was she about to accept? Seb forced his mind carefully into neutral, trying to suppress panic at the thought that she might refuse. To lose so much...

But there was also fear of what lay ahead if she said yes. Marriage.

No. House sharing, he told himself. Independence. It couldn't work any other way. But when the ferry reached the island and she was outside the terminal waiting for him, the qualms he'd been trying to suppress at the thought of marriage came flooding back.

Why did the sight of her make him feel...as he had no right to feel?

She was wearing shorts and a frayed T-shirt, her sun-bleached hair still looked like it could do with a good comb and her long, tanned legs looked like they went on for ever.

She was leaning against a beach buggy that looked ancient, as did the battered surfboard strapped on its rollbars. But even though she looked scruffy and the vehicle she was driving looked as if it was almost ready for the scrapyard, the way she looked… Weirdly, it made him feel amazing. That this woman was waiting for him… That she was smiling and waving, straight at him…

And she was here to talk marriage?

'Hey,' he said as he met her. And then, because he felt like his entire body was clenched in readiness for a verdict, he asked directly, 'What's the decision?'

'Not here. We need to go somewhere private.' And she refused to speak again, just shook her head and motioned to the passenger seat.

The silence continued as they drove. The need to know was hammering in his head but she seemed intent on her driving. Finally, she turned off the main road onto a sandy track, then pulled up at the entrance to a cove which seemed both secluded and lovely.

'This island has ears everywhere and I don't want us to be disturbed,' she said briefly as she parked. She produced a picnic blanket from the back, spread it out on the sand, then fetched a basket containing coffee and a packet of biscuits. She sat down, opened the biscuits and poured coffee. Then, as he was still standing, feeling bemused, she came right out with it.

'Okay, Seb. Bottom line is that I'll marry you. But with conditions.'

Whoa. To say he was hornswoggled would have

been an understatement. He was about to be married. How did that make him feel?

Panicked, he conceded. Very, very panicked.

'Conditions?' he managed, and was surprised that his voice actually worked.

'Arthur threw conditions at us,' she told him. 'We can surely throw a few back.' She held out a coffee. 'Sit.'

He sat and she proffered her biscuits. 'Tim Tams,' she told him, her voice amazingly steady, given the circumstances. 'These are my favourite biscuits, especially through coffee. Are they yours? I suspect that should be one of our marriage conditions. If you don't like Tim Tams we're clearly incompatible.' Then she bit off two diagonally opposite corners of her biscuit, stuck one end in her coffee and proceeded to use it like a straw.

What was happening here? He'd arrived thinking this would be a businesslike discussion—and they were sitting on the beach eating Tim Tams.

And there was the lesser—surely lesser?—fact that this woman was starting to seem…gorgeous. Had she been gorgeous the first time he'd seen her? She'd been battered and weary, he'd hardly taken in what she was wearing, but she *had* made an impression. Or more than an impression.

Had Arthur seen the same thing? Was that why he…?

No. That was too deep. He shook his head, trying to clear confusion, but confusion refused to be cleared.

Marriage?

'Did you really just say yes?' he said faintly, and she looked at him in surprise. She lifted what remained of her Tim Tam out of her coffee, half biscuit, half oozing melted chocolate, and popped it all into her mouth. And focused. Her eyes said bliss.

She had him fascinated.

'I really did say yes,' she managed when it was finally gone. 'I swear these are nectar of the gods. When life gets complicated, Tim Tams and coffee—or Tim Tams and hot chocolate—are the only answer. This scheme seems complicated enough to warrant all three.'

'Is this a discussion of marriage or an advertisement?' he asked, still befuddled.

'I just thought…how long since you've done this? Sat on a beach and eaten whatever you wanted? I've done some major research on you now, Seb Cantrell, and your lifestyle sounds appalling. I apologise for implying you were as much a waste of space as I am.'

'I never implied that you…'

She cut him off. 'Of course you did. What was your proposal? That I come to Brisbane and spend a couple of years surfing and spending a million dollars? As if I'd be happy doing that. But to a

certain extent I agree. I don't take life seriously.'
She shrugged. 'But you...how often do you surf?'

What sort of a question was this when so much
was at stake?

'Not often,' he confessed. 'In fact, not for years.
But I was surfing the day my uncle was injured.
I accused him of never enjoying himself, and
then...'

'And then you both decided to surf? But before
then? Or since?'

'Um...what's this got to do with marriage?'

She shot him a strange look. 'Hey, am I wasting your time discussing details? Do you want to
go straight to the register office?'

'Jodie...'

'Yeah, I know.' She shrugged again. 'This is serious. The whole thing's ridiculously serious. But I
have done my due diligence, and you're right, there
doesn't seem much choice but for me to marry
you.'

What? Had she just said 'I do'? Was he about
to be *married* to this...beach nymph?

'There's a romantic acceptance,' he managed,
feeling winded. Or feeling more than winded. It
wouldn't be a real marriage, he told himself a trifle desperately. Not a real commitment. She was
agreeing to sign a piece of paper. She wasn't prom-
ising to commit long-term.

He wouldn't have to commit either.

She'd gone back to concentrating on the next

Tim Tam. He watched her eat in silence until finally she sighed, put down her empty mug and faced him head-on.

'It's not romantic, is it, and that's what I've figured,' she said bluntly, her gaze locked on his. 'So let's get this straight. You're suggesting we marry, I live with you in Brisbane, I get some sort of job over there—not that I'll need to, according to you. You're proposing that I can be as frivolous as I like, while you get on with saving the world.'

'That's an overstatement.'

'But essentially correct?'

'Jodie, I don't see how else it can work,' he told her, fighting back emotions he was struggling to understand. 'I can't go back to Al Delebe, but I'll need to be in Brisbane, to keep up my skills, but also to focus on company matters. You have no idea of the complexities of changing the direction of such an enormous corporation. I still don't know how I'll do it.' He paused and gestured out towards the beach—the beckoning waves, the sunlight glinting through the palms. 'So I can't afford to do this.'

'But my condition is that you'll have to.'

'Have to what?'

'Stay here. On Kirra.'

'How can I do that? My work is in…'

'Brisbane. No, it's not. Not all of it. Seb, I get what you need, but this marriage can't be a one-way deal. I need to focus on me.'

'You'll get a million…'

And that produced silence. He saw her eyes flash with something he didn't understand—but suddenly he did. Her anger was almost tangible.

'You know, if you say one more word about payment I might get back in the buggy and drive away,' she said at last, very, very carefully. 'You can get back to the ferry whatever way you like, but you'll do it alone.'

'It's not payment. It's…'

'Shut up. I'm not kidding. Enough of me being a wastrel, a layabout. Without being insulting, are you prepared to listen to my part of the deal?'

Was she implying the money wasn't important? A million dollars? It surely had to be, but she was moving on.

'I told you, I've been doing some research,' she told him. 'And a lot of thinking. The work you're doing for Al Delebe can surely mostly be done online. You'll need to cut down your public presentations, but for the sake of Al Delebe's future, with your uncle's entire legacy at stake, surely the cost/benefit breakdown will be worth it.'

'But…'

'Shut up and listen,' she told him quite kindly. 'You're also currently doing clinical work three days a week and one weekend in three. I've thought that through, and I see no reason why you can't continue. Lots of islanders use the ferry to commute. You could leave here at seven in the morning, get to Brisbane at eight, leave Brisbane at six at night and get back here by seven. Or there's a company helicopter. Your uncle used it. I don't see why you can't.'

'But the work I do…'

She held up her hands as if to stop him, realised two fingers were covered in chocolate and obviously decided they needed to be licked. She proceeded to lick, then carefully wiped them on a napkin before proceeding.

'I do realise there might be the occasional need to stay,' she admitted. 'Sometimes with surgery you need to be on hand for complications, but Brisbane Central has overnight accommodation for medical staff. I think the marriage boundaries can stretch to the occasional night apart. I assume there'll be meetings with your corporation people too, lots of meetings. You can go back and forth to Brisbane if you must, or hold them online here.'

Whoa. He stared at her, stunned. 'You really have been researching…'

'This is marriage. Why wouldn't I research?'

'But why do we need to stay on the island?'

'Because,' she said slowly, 'contrary to what you think, I do care. I came here as a part-time locum but it's become my home. Misty's about to have a baby, which means the island would essentially be left with one doctor. Besides, I'm not doing this all on your terms. A quick wedding in a register office and then off to live a life of indolence in your fancy apartment? I don't think so. Oh, and speaking of weddings...'

'Weddings?' He was feeling dazed.

'Marriages require weddings,' she said. Her flash of anger had gone and she was now even managing to sound cheerful. 'And if we go through with this, I want a big one. Huge.'

He blinked. 'You're kidding.'

'Nope.'

'But it's not a real marriage.'

'Of course it's not, but I don't see why it can't be a real wedding. We...the islanders...have had a couple of bad fishing seasons, and the recent storm caused major damage. We could use some cheering up.'

She hesitated but then continued. 'Seb, everything I've read in this contract is all about you, and the company, and the good you can do. I acknowledge your work is save-the-world-important. But I only have one little life, and that's important to me, too. So I've decided, if I'm indeed part of this equation then I need to stick with what makes me get up in the morning.'

'Which is?'

'Surfing,' she said tentatively, and then at the look on his face she held up her hands. 'I know, there it is again. You think that's a waste of space, and maybe it is, but it holds my head together. And teaching kids surfing is great too. It gives me joy.'

'You can't just...'

'But that's not all,' she cut in. 'Two years ago I would have said surfing was my passion, medicine was my job and there was little else. But I've been on this island for a while now. I came to help a friend but I ended up staying, and its inhabitants…well, somehow, they've become part of who I am. Seb, as a kid, a teen, even into early adulthood, I felt like a drifter. A loner. You don't need to hear about it and I don't need to tell you, apart from saying moving to this island, growing closer to these people, has made my life seem more… solid. I'm not sure if you can understand that, but if this wedding will give everyone pleasure…'

'Jodie…'

'Don't you dare say saving the sight of so many people should be a bigger reason,' she said. 'I accept how important it is, and if still living here would prevent that then I might even change my mind. But I don't see how it would. You can work yourself into the ground as easily here as in Brisbane. So, what do you think?'

She paused then and waited while he tried to think of how to respond. To move here… To live here properly… To become part of a community, even if only for two years… Why did that seem like some sort of chasm where he couldn't see the bottom?

But now Jodie was frowning, her gaze intensifying.

'Speaking of your work,' she said slowly. 'Your

workload seems crazy, and…are you okay? Have you lost weight since I last saw you?'

'Hardly. It's only been a week.'

'No, I meant over the last few months. You look…' she stared at him, obviously concerned '…a bit…drawn?'

'I'm fine. Jodie, I can't live here.'

'Take it or leave it,' she said bluntly, her gaze still intent. 'I guess worrying about what's facing you might put anyone off their food. But you haven't even eaten a Tim Tam.'

'I had sandwiches on the ferry.'

'What sort of excuse is that?' But she gave a small nod, as if telling herself to move on—that his weight was none of her business? 'Seb, I would like you to see just a glimpse of what's important to me. I brought you here to show you this beach, to show you one source of my love for this place, and now, if you'll allow me, I'll show you another.'

'Another beach?'

'A patient,' she told him. 'Mrs Isabelle Grundy. Ninety-four years old. Six kids, more than a dozen grandkids and heaven knows how many great-grandies. I asked if I might bring another doctor when I visit her today and she reacted with delight. If you have enough energy with no Tim Tams on board…'

'Of course I have. Let's go.' He felt as if he was being railroaded, and saw her smile return.

'Feeling out of control?' she asked. 'Well, that's

how I've been feeling for the last week, and if we're talking marriage then sharing's surely part of it. Welcome to my world.'

Isabelle Grundy had lived her entire life on the island. Her father had been a fisherman, her husband had been a fisherman and now so were four of her adult children and six of her grandkids. She lived in a tiny cottage overlooking the harbour.

'By herself?' Seb asked as she outlined Isabelle's background and condition.

'Of course by herself. She wouldn't have it any other way.'

'But what you tell me…'

'Yep, advanced pancreatic cancer, crippling arthritis, general debilitation—she should be in a nursing home, right? Her kids and grandkids are in and out, though, and if there's anything she needs…well, her cottage is great. You'll see.'

They were outside the cottage. Jodie knocked and a 'Hooroo…' echoed from above.

'Door's not locked,' an old voice called. 'Did you bring your doc friend?'

'I did,' Jodie called back. 'Are you respectable?'

'I got Maureen to get me a new nightie,' she called back. 'Just in case.'

Bemused, Seb followed Jodie up a narrow flight of stairs. The house was tiny, one room up, one room down.

'She didn't raise her family here?' he asked, and Jodie shook her head.

'They had a bigger place further up the hill, but when the kids left and her husband died she swapped to this one.'

'It's hardly suitable. These stairs…'

And then Jodie pushed open the bedroom door and he changed his mind about what was suitable.

The room was small but his eyes were immediately drawn to its window, which was wide, double-hung and overlooking the harbour below. And not just the harbour. You could almost see to Brisbane, he thought, awed, and then realised that both Isabelle and Jodie were looking at him and grinning.

'I told you he'd like it,' Jodie said, and Isabelle chuckled. It was a weak chuckle—the old lady's eyes, sunk into a gaunt face, spoke of serious long-term illness, but it was still infectious, even cheerful.

As was her bedroom. The room was simply furnished, most of it taken up by an old-fashioned double bed, pushed hard against the window. Isabelle, obviously small to begin with and now wizened with age, seemed almost dwarfed by her surroundings. A litter of magazines, balls of knitting wool and a half-finished…scarf?…were scattered across a gaily coloured patchwork quilt. Three cats, two tabby, one ginger, were regarding the newcomers with benevolent caution. They'd been snoozing in a beam of sunshine and their combined look said, *Disturb us at your peril.*

'You like my nightie?' Isabelle, propped up on pillows, was demanding this of Jodie, but her eyes were blatantly assessing Seb.

'It's great,' Jodie told her, eyeing the pink and lavender, high-necked and frilled nightwear with appreciation.

'Maureen went to Brisbane yesterday. I gave her instructions, and she went to four places to find it. Pretty, huh? So, are you going to introduce us?'

'Isabelle, this is Dr Cantrell. Is it okay if he stays?'

'Of course he can stay,' she retorted and turned to Seb. 'Do you like my nightie?'

'It's fabulous,' he told her honestly, and Jodie grinned.

'So, tell me…' Isabelle started but Jodie cut across her.

'Isabelle, before you start grilling Seb on his life story, could you tell me what's happening with you. Pain level?'

'Six,' Isabelle said, not taking her eyes from Seb.

Ouch. In a range of one to ten, six was pretty much unbearable.

'Then we need to adjust your syringe driver,' Jodie told her, and that made Seb notice the up-to-date medical apparatus around them.

'You have a syringe driver?' he asked incredulously. 'Do you have in-home nursing care?'

'We have everything we need,' Jodie told him, perching on the bed and lifting Isabelle's wrist. 'And the family's back and forth.'

'But no one stays here?'

'Jacob, Isabelle's son, lives just down the road, Maureen lives around the corner and both the neighbours are friends. These cottages are jammed right against each other and if Isabelle needs help in the night all she needs to do is thump her cane on the wall.'

'But…'

'Oi! No buts!' Isabelle's voice was thin but firm. 'Last time I saw the doc in Brisbane he said I'll die soon, and I'm ready. He wanted me to stay in hospital and he couldn't take responsibility if anything happened to me at home, but I said, "What's the worst that can happen?"'

'And this is surely the best,' Jodie said warmly. 'You and your family are great. But that pain's up. Let's see the cocktail.' She outlined the dosage running through the driver. 'What do you think?' she asked Seb.

He was an ophthalmologist. This wasn't his field—surely a pain specialist was what she needed—but Jodie was looking at him expectantly. And he did know pain—from both sides, doctor and patient.

'You might up the morphine,' he said diffi- dently, and she shook her head.

'She'll take nothing that'll make her drowsy.'

'Two of my grandkids are at sea,' Isabelle told him, still watching him with interest. 'Boats are coming in at dusk. I need to check their catch.'

'They'll unload just below the cottage,' Josie said, and Isabelle nodded.

'That's right, and Maureen might bring me a nice bit of snapper for my tea. Fresh off the boat, and what's a bit of pain compared to missing that?'

He had to agree.

And he also saw why Jodie had brought him here. For a woman like this to be able to stay in her own home, to not need to spend the last weeks of her life in a hospital far away from those she loved... Okay, maybe it wasn't a saving-the-world calling, but he couldn't deny its worth.

He couldn't deny what Jodie was giving to this community.

He watched while Jodie asked gentle questions, carefully examined, did everything in her power to make her comfortable. Then, as she made a call to a pain specialist in Brisbane, he sat on the bed and let Isabelle talk. She had him fascinated, but in turn she also seemed intrigued. Within minutes she'd learned about Al Delebe and her questions were intelligent and interested.

'You not going back?' she demanded.

'I can't,' he said regretfully. 'I've had dengue fever.'

And she obviously knew about dengue and its risks too. This seemed one intelligent woman.

'Bugger,' she said and then she brightened. 'But that means you can stay.' She paused for a moment, obviously considering the implications. 'He looks a good 'un,' she told Jodie when she'd finished her call. 'You going to try and keep him here?'

'I'll try,' Jodie said. 'But first there's a couple of things he needs to agree are of value. Like helping you stay here instead of hospital. What do you reckon that's worth, Isabelle?'

'The blasted world,' she said stoutly and then she fixed Seb with a beady stare. 'So… This is a great place and Doc Jodie…she's the best. You married?'

'I… No.'

'Then there's a solution. Marry Jodie, settle on the island, have a few kids and live happily ever after. Sixty or so years from now I'll tell the kids you can rent this bed for your passing. How good would that be? What do you say?'

What did he say? Both women were watching him, seemingly waiting for a decision.

'I'm not so sure about the bed,' he said cautiously. 'Its springs might be sagging a bit by then.'

And then he looked at Jodie and discovered her

eyes were dancing. Had she set this up? Of course she had.

So...was this decision time? Was he about to commit to giving up his life in Brisbane?

But he wouldn't be totally giving it up, he realised, and he thought about taking Jodie away from this—how could he ask that of her? Even for a million...

And marriage... He was getting deeper and deeper. He thought of Arthur and his Machiavellian scheme. Family. Commitment.

To a woman called Jodie. To a woman whose presence alone seemed enough to unsettle his ordered world.

But there seemed no choice and Jodie and Isabelle were both waiting for him to answer. So finally...finally he raised an eyebrow towards Jodie in an unspoken question. She grinned and nodded. *Go ahead*, her smile said, obviously knowing exactly where his thoughts were headed. And her eyes twinkled straight at him.

And the way that made him feel...

What a step to take, he thought, but Jodie's look was warm and teasing and suddenly the step didn't seem so huge. Even...desirable?

Whoa, he thought, one step at a time. But the first step seemed about to be taken.

Why not?

'I guess you might as well be the first to know,' he told Isabelle. 'I've asked Jodie to marry me.'

The old lady's eyes widened so much they almost enveloped her face, but Seb wasn't looking at her. He was looking at Jodie.

Her eyes were still smiling.

Where was this landing him? He had no idea but right now, standing by this lady's bed, looking at Jodie's smile, all he could do was smile back. And the way it made him feel… The chasm before him suddenly seemed…like a siren song?

'Has she said yes?' Isabelle's delight was palpable.

'Can we stay on the island?' Jodie asked, still smiling.

'Of course.' It was the sensible course, he told himself but the frisson of whatever that siren song contained seemed to be growing.

'Then yes,' Jodie said, and Isabelle gave a whoop of excitement.

'Really? Was that a real proposal? Do you two want to kiss?'

'No,' they said, totally in unison, and Isabelle's eyes danced with approval.

'You want to do it in private? I can close my eyes, but it's done and accepted and that's all that matters. Can I come to your wedding?'

'Of course,' he said, feeling as if he was acting on automatic pilot. Marriage. A wedding. But there was no choice.

And Jodie was still smiling. 'If you can stay

alive long enough, why on earth not? No promises, but let's see if we can make that happen.'

'Ooh.' Weakness forgotten, Isabelle was all excitement. 'Will the wedding be big? Can all the islanders come, like at Angus and Misty's? And oh, I have a cute little pattern for bride and groom knitted rabbits. I made them for Maureen's wedding and we put them on top of their wedding cake. Two white rabbits, one with a veil, the other with a top hat. She and Geoff still have them on their mantelpiece. They have brown feet now, though,' she said with a hint of disapproval. 'I never knew the cake was going to be chocolate and they can't get the stains out. What colour's your cake going to be?'

'I have no idea,' Jodie said faintly.

'Well, there's lots of ideas,' Isabelle told them, moving on. 'I'll get Dot to order in bridal magazines and we'll have a look. Dot's a pretty good cook, too. It'll have to be big, but she could bake it and you could get Lionel to ice it. You know he did Maureen's? And Misty and Angus's. But no chocolate.'

'No chocolate,' she promised faintly.

'And what do you reckon my chances are of living long enough to make you some baby clothes?' she asked.

Baby clothes? *What?* No!

'No baby clothes,' he decreed, and Isabelle pouted.

'What, not ever?'

Not ever? He thought of his uncle's will, and then he looked at Jodie and there was a flash of something he didn't understand.

She'd been smiling, caught up in Isabelle's excitement, but now the laughter had gone. Was that fear?

'Enough,' she said, almost roughly, and bent over her bag—to put equipment away or to disguise emotion? When she lifted her face again the fear was gone, her smile was back, but it seemed forced. 'One step at a time,' she told Isabelle firmly. 'For now...'

'Let's just concentrate on rabbits?' Isabelle asked cheekily.

And Jodie said, 'Why not?' Then she kissed her on the cheek and ushered her now-fiancé out of the room.

Then there were details to be sorted, and for a while emotion took a back step. They drove back to Jodie's, they sat on the veranda and went through what needed to happen, point by point.

They were both strained, both unsure of where to go from here, so all they could do was be businesslike.

'If we need to be together for two years, we may as well get it over with as fast as possible,' Jodie told him and he agreed.

The minimum time it took to register their intention to marry with the authorities—and for Isa-belle to knit rabbits—seemed a good idea to them both. One month.

Then the details.

He asked—very tentatively—how many is-landers would like to come. She thought maybe a couple of hundred. He nodded, as if this was to-tally normal. He figured his list was about ten—including lawyers. She smiled perfunctorily and her reply was clipped.

'The weather should still be great, and it'll be outside,' she said stiffly. 'The islanders should enjoy it.'

'Will you?' he asked, and she stared into the middle distance and seemed to consider.

'Maybe I will,' she said at last, with a tension behind her words that he didn't understand. Or maybe he did—maybe he was feeling the same.

'I'll try,' she said at last. 'When I was a little girl, I used to dream about a fairy tale wedding—a princess dress, a tiara, a floaty veil, flowers, flow-ers and more flowers. I pretty much gave up that dream but…well, why not?'

'Why did you give it up?' he asked curiously, and her face closed.

'I grew up,' she said shortly. 'Don't we all? But maybe…'

'Maybe the princess dress might be fun?' he ventured, thinking why not? 'The estate will cover it. You won't need to cut into your million.'

'As if that's a factor,' she said, suddenly grim. 'Screw your million, Seb Cantrell.'

He looked at her oddly. 'Jodie, you need to know, no matter what the cost, at the end of this marriage you will walk away with…'

'I said shut up,' she snapped, really angry now. 'I refuse to go into this thinking I'm being bought.'

'You mean you don't want…'

'Okay, maybe I do,' she admitted, but grudgingly. 'But I hate that I want. I can surely use a million but I'd have accepted without. It's not a deal breaker.' She closed her eyes for a moment and then visibly moved on. 'Okay. Flower girls, pageboys, a fairy tale wedding—that should silence your lawyers. What I want won't come into it.'

But then she managed a rueful smile. 'But okay, maybe I *would* love the excuse, for once in my life, to shop for a fairy tale wedding dress. Misty and I will have fun. So next… Living arrangements? Here's good.'

'Here?' He looked around him at the worn little beach shack and thought…really?

'Let me show you.'

And as she led him through her home, he thought why not? There were two bedrooms, one big enough to hold a decent desk.

'This can be yours,' she told him. 'I can do any desk work at the clinic.' A light-filled living-room-cum-kitchen looked over the bay. There was a serviceable bathroom, a veranda, a washing machine on the deck and that was it. 'What else do we need?' she asked, and she looked at him almost defiantly.

He thought of his luxurious unit in Brisbane and then he thought of the rough hut he'd used as living quarters in Al Delebe.

'This is great,' he said, and she shot him a disbelieving glance but nodded.

'It should work. Short of having a team of lawyers watching on our wedding night—and if you say that's required then I'm out of here—we're doing everything we can.'

'It's not required,' he said faintly. 'At least, I don't think so.'

'Then check,' she said firmly. 'Two bedrooms, Seb Cantrell, and that's that. Your room's big. You can ship over a decent desk, maybe an armchair, a telly. We can share meals...'

'You don't think we can watch telly together?'

'Maybe,' she conceded, still stiffly. 'Tell me what you like and we'll discuss it. But Scandi Noir's off the table, as is every single show that involves body parts.'

He managed a smile but he felt dazed and that feeling continued as they proceeded to discuss dates, times and details. Finally, she dropped him off at the ferry, deal done.

Finished?

But as they pulled into the car park they realised

the news had already spread. Obviously, Isabelle had sent out carrier pigeons. They were met by surely more islanders than would normally use the ferry. Word was obviously out that this man was a doctor, that he was about to marry *their* Doc Jodie, and he was coming to the island to live. So, what was there not to like? They were surrounded by well-wishers.

Once aboard though, he was left alone. He sat in the bow and thought...*what's there not to like?*

He thought of Jodie, standing stiffly among the ferry passengers as she'd said farewell, the congratulations around them obviously messing with her head.

He should have kissed her, he thought, and as he'd said goodbye there'd been an urge to do just that. But somehow he'd sensed that if he had, she'd have backed right off. Maybe even pulled out of the deal?

What had gone on in her background? He'd researched the basics but he needed to know more. He had a sudden urge to demand the ferry turned around, for him to take time, to figure out what was making her tick. To see if he could remove the shadows that caused those intermittent flashes of fear.

But the ferry wouldn't turn, and even if it could he didn't have time. He had to get back, see the lawyers, start the mind-blowing legal process that'd mean he could take charge of the Cantrell mines.

The thought was doing his head in. The thought of everything was doing his head in.

What he wanted, he thought desperately as the island disappeared in the distance, was to be back in Al Delebe, in the operating theatre, making a difference. But there was also a part of him admitting what he'd really like was to stay on the island tonight, to get to know this woman he was about to marry.

But there'll be two years, a voice in the back of his head murmured, thinking again of her stiffness, of her fear.

This is business only, he reminded himself.

It had to be only business.

He was suddenly thinking of his parents, consumed by their passion to save sight, impressing him over and over with their mantra.

'You're on this earth to do good, Seb. Nothing should get in the way of that. Nothing.'

Jodie shouldn't get in the way.

But still there were whispers of something growing louder.

Jodie. Two years.

Two years to do good—in all sorts of ways?

And Jodie? She watched the ferry disappear into the distance and thought, what have I done?

Promised to marry.

Promised to share her home.

Promised to share her life?

The thought left her scared witless. Since she'd been fifteen she'd been alone—or maybe even before that. She'd fought her own fights; she'd dealt with life on her own terms and she'd depended on no one.

'This doesn't mean I'll depend on him,' she told herself. 'He'll be living here on my terms. I can treat him like a boarder, nothing more. And hey, I can buy a dress.'

The thought almost distracted her. She was a jeans and T-shirt woman, or shorts and T-shirt, or skirt and dead plain shirt for work. She used the hairdresser once every six months to cope with split ends. She had a toilet bag that contained toothbrush, hairbrush, a huge tub of sunscreen and not much else. So why had the fantasy of a fairy tale dress suddenly slipped into her head?

Her parents would love it, she thought, and for a moment she let herself play with the idea of phoning them, which would be the first time she'd done such a thing in over fifteen years.

'Hey, parents, I'm respectable again and next month I'm marrying one of the richest men in Australia. You want to come to the wedding?'

They might even come, she thought. They might even decide their 'filthy little tart' of a daughter had redeemed herself. She could be their daughter again.

'But I haven't redeemed myself,' she said out loud, regardless of the guys setting up their fishing rods on the jetty now the ferry had left. 'Somewhere there's my daughter, and wherever she is I'm proud of her.'

Hali.

Oh, God, would she ever forget?

'I've just agreed to marry one of the richest, and surely one of the most gorgeous, males in this country,' she told herself angrily as she turned and headed back to the beach buggy, fighting back stupid, useless tears. 'Why can't I stop thinking of Hali?'

Because…

Because this seemed a betrayal?

'And that makes no sort of sense,' she told herself. 'You're not moving on. You're not planning on babies, of replacing…'

Yeah, that was dumb.

'Business only,' she told herself. And that million?

It would make a difference.

'So Seb's saving one part of the world and I'll be saving a little bit,' she said, still out loud, as she climbed into her beach buggy. 'Nothing else matters—but I will buy a dress, and damn them all.'

CHAPTER SEVEN

Four weeks later

SEB STOOD ON the headland and waited for his bride.

This wedding had become almost bigger than the cast of *Ben-Hur*. A colossus.

The islanders had reacted to the news with incredulous delight. When Jodie had confirmed, almost sheepishly, that she was about to marry someone who was bound to become one of the country's richest men, and he was intending to live here, they'd assumed the wedding would be an invitation-only, celebrity-heavy affair. When Jodie had said no, the wedding was to be on the headland, everyone was welcome, and who wanted to be a flower girl or pageboy? they'd been mind-blown.

'Because why shouldn't everyone enjoy it?' Jodie had asked the dumbfounded Misty. 'It's not as if I'm doing this for me. Let's open it right up.'

And why not? There'd been no way they could keep it quiet, and if Seb was to use this as a means to take control of one of Australia's largest corporations it had to be public knowledge.

So the islanders had come on board. When Seb had arrived the night before the wedding, Jodie had taken him on a tour of the venue—a gorgeous swathe of grassland on the bluff overlooking the sea, edged on three sides by gumtrees filled with noisy lorikeets settling down for the night. The locals had set up what must have been every spare chair on the island. They'd set up an arch with a backdrop of sweeping ocean and they'd covered it with flowers, flowers and more flowers. The entire setting was spectacular.

'Gorgeous, huh?' Jodie had told him and, to his astonishment, she didn't sound nervous—she sounded as if she was enjoying herself. 'But I can't believe you won't have anyone with you other than Angus.'

He hadn't wanted anyone. His life had been so intense until now that no one was close enough to expect to be part of the ceremony.

He had met Angus, though. Misty's husband, the other island doctor, had come across to Brisbane especially to meet him and, to Seb's bemusement, the meeting had turned out to be pretty much a grilling on his 'intentions'. It seemed Jodie was to be protected. The questioning had been intense, but in the end Angus had relaxed. Seb had taken time off to have a beer with the guy and they figured they had the beginnings of a tentative friendship. So as best man...

'He's all I need,' he'd declared. 'Why do we need attendants anyway?'

'Because it's fun,' Jodie had replied. 'Though I

guess any attendant you choose wouldn't exactly be heading to the internet to find pink tulle and glitter.'

'Is that what your attendants will be wearing?' he'd asked faintly, and she'd grinned.

'You'd better believe it.'

So now...

He was standing under the arch, Angus by his side, wondering how on earth he'd ever got himself into this...fantasy?

For that was what it was, he told himself as the music swelled, as hundreds of islanders rose to their feet, as the bridal procession finally arrived.

And what a bridal procession.

She hadn't been kidding when she'd said that any child could be part of this. Here they came, what, twenty or thirty kids?

When Jodie had told him her plan, he'd expected a bevy of little girls, but she'd put it out there—any child who'd like to be part of her procession was welcome to come, dressed as anything they liked, but the theme was fantasy. So there was a mass of pink tulle but there were also... Space Invaders? Supermen? Superwomen? Medieval knights? The only stipulation—decreed by Misty rather than Jodie, he gathered—was that every partici-pating kid should carry flowers, any shape, any way they wanted.

So now they filed along the flower-strewn aisle, in rows of three, intent on carrying this out with all solemnity, walking in time with Handel's Water Music, played by the local string quartet. A mass of kids and fantasy and flowers, reaching the arch, smiling beatifically and then laying their flowers down to further mark the makeshift aisle for Jodie to walk along.

Then they scattered to sit beside their parents, and Jodie was standing alone.

He'd thought she'd have Misty beside her but no. Misty had been there, behind the kids, but she too had edged back. She was now sitting in the front row beside Isabelle Grundy, who was in her wheelchair, beaming as if she'd organised this whole wedding herself.

So Jodie walked the flower-strewn aisle by herself.

And she took his breath away.

This wasn't the Jodie he knew—or sort of knew. This, too, was fantasy. Her dress was all gold and glitter. The bodice seemed sculpted to her breasts and waist. The scooped neck was edged with gold embroidery, diamonds—surely fake! Three-quarter-length sleeves seemed also moulded as if she was sewn into the garment, and at the waist the dress flared out in a glorious circle of white and gold, with a train stretching out behind.

Her sun-blonde hair was coifed and curled, and a glinting diamanté tiara nestled in her locks. Wide blue eyes smiled out at the world and he thought, surely those have to be fake lashes? And surely this was professional make-up? He'd only ever seen her in work clothes or the simple gear she used as casual but now she seemed almost ethereal. A fairy princess. Every little girl in the gathered crowd was beaming with delight.

A fairy princess. His fairy princess? Certainly his bride. She walked steadily towards him and she was smiling. He caught that smile and smiled back. But why was his overwhelming impression suddenly that of loneliness?

And suddenly, inexplicably, he knew that what was happening here was a form of protection.

This was a mock ceremony. This wasn't real, so why not make it something out of a fairy story? Cinderella with her prince? Sleeping Beauty? A story where the fantasy wedding ended with the words 'They lived happily ever after' and then the book was closed.

So this book would be closed after today, he thought. He'd be a boarder in her cottage, and she'd stay as the solitary woman she'd always been.

Always?

What was behind that mask? Who was this woman—this ethereal princess bride who smiled and smiled, but whose smile couldn't quite disguise fear?

She reached his side and he held out his hand to take hers. There was a moment's pause and he glanced at her and thought, Is this why the make-up? To disguise a white face? To hide terror?

'This is okay,' he said softly, holding her gaze. 'I won't intrude on your space, I promise. You're still your own woman, Jodie Tavish.'

She blinked and he saw astonishment. There was a long moment while their eyes held.

'We'll do good,' he said, so softly that no one but them could hear. 'But we'll do it apart. This is pretend, to save the world, so we might as well get on with it. What do you say?'

'I… Yes.'

'And it might even be fun,' he said, his smile encouraging her to smile back. 'That's some gown. You should have told me; I would have come as a medieval knight. Maybe without the armour though.' And then he hesitated. 'But I'm thinking… Jodie, I trust you and I hope I don't need armour. Will you trust me as well?'

And there was a long pause while almost the entire island seemed to hold its breath. And finally the look of fear eased off.

'I do,' she whispered, and somehow she managed to smile back—and then they turned to make 'I do' official.

What followed was the party to end all parties, and Jodie even found herself enjoying it.

When she'd first suggested this idea to Misty it had boggled her mind—and then she'd been overwhelmingly enthusiastic. Together they'd taken their tentative plan to the island's community leaders. The recent storm that had battered the island so badly had cast a pall. Every gathering since seemed to have been a fundraiser to help those most badly affected.

'This is just what we need to cheer everyone up,' Misty had declared. 'We'll have it out on the headland where there's little damage and we'll have fun!'

And they did have fun. A feast to end all feasts—contributions from almost everyone. Jumping castles, jugglers, acrobats—everyone who could do anything was invited to do their bit. There was even a fortune-teller, for heaven's sake, and laughingly the islanders insisted the bride and groom be first to have theirs told.

So in a rainbow-covered tent, full of crystals and incense and make-believe, they sat hand in hand while a gloriously gowned Mystic Marigold—alias Dot Hemming, postmistress—predicted a hundred-year marriage blessed with twelve children and a dog.

Jodie even found herself relaxing enough to giggle. If this whole two years could be treated as fantasy she could get through it, she told herself. She wasn't losing her independence. She wasn't!

'You'd think if she can predict twelve kids she might have predicted twelve dogs,' Seb grumbled as they left the tent. 'One dog's never going to last the distance.'

'Why not a unicorn or two as well?' she asked. 'Honestly, I'm feeling short-changed.'

He chuckled and the tension eased. This might even be okay. They could be business partners. Friends. She could do friends.

But then, as the sun's shadows lengthened, as the local band decreed it was time for the bridal waltz, as Seb took his princess bride into his arms and whirled her round the makeshift dance floor— who would ever have guessed he could dance like this?—she found herself...melting?

Melting? No. What was the word?

Once upon a time one of her aunts had run a ballroom dance studio in the small outback town where she'd been raised. She remembered her uncle coaching her to move with him, schooling her to dance as one, so as Seb held her and led her into the waltz, her feet moved with almost muscle memory.

He was surely a better dancer than her uncle— and he definitely felt better.

He looked gorgeous—or was gorgeous too small a word?—in a deep black dinner suit, crisp linen shirt and a black tie flecked with tiny gold specks. Misty must have given it to him, she thought. Misty had helped choose her dress and she might have organised his tie to match. But now, held in his arms, twirling across the floor, matching his every move with instinctive sureness, feeling his strength and skill, she thought, no, this man would have chosen his own tie.

It was an odd thing to think, but strangely it brought back the fear. She must have faltered because he pulled back a little so he could see her face.

'Jodie?'

It was a question. He knew all wasn't right with her and the question disturbed her still more.

'It's okay,' she managed. 'More…more than okay.'

'I think it can be,' he told her and then he smiled, that heart-stopping smile that did something to her insides she had no hope of controlling. 'And right now I'm thinking it might be more than okay. Let's just relax, my bride, and go with the music.'

And what was there in that to make her even more panicked?

They headed back to her cottage…*their* cottage?… at midnight, clattering back in her beach buggy, the clattering caused by the mass of old boots and tin cans tied to the bumper bar.

Jodie drove, somehow bunching up her bridal dress and squashing it into the footwell. Seb sat silently beside her. After the clamour of the crowd shouting their farewells there seemed nothing to say. The vastness of what had happened seemed to be overwhelming.

The cottage seemed strangely still in the moonlight, far away from the music, laughter and chaos of the day. They sat for a moment as she cut the engine, staring out at the scene before them. The moon was hanging low in the sky over the sea. They could hear the faint hush hush of the surf. Otherwise, the silence was absolute. Not even an owl or a scrambling bush turkey disturbed the stillness.

'I'm going in to take off this dress,' Jodie said at last. 'It weighs a ton. I can't wait to get it off.'

'Fairy tale ended?' he asked, turning to face her in the moonlight. He hadn't come close to figuring her out yet. She was obviously a beloved member of this community, a skilled and caring doctor, and yet all this day he'd thought she seemed so alone.

Why was his sense of her isolation deepening rather than weakening? Even during the waltz… At times he'd felt her body melt against his and then, almost in a panicked reaction, there'd been stiffening, until somehow she'd forced herself to relax again.

What was behind the fear? He'd told her his background, yet he knew almost nothing about her.

Oh, he knew the basics. The moment he'd read his great-uncle's will he'd done a search—of course he had.

Jodie Tavish. Born in Conburrawong, a small town some two hundred kilometres west of Brisbane. Parents, Brian and Evelyn, Brian a pharmacist, Evelyn a librarian. Stalwarts of the local church. Part-time scout leaders, full time leaders of the Conburrawong Tidy Towns committee. Jodie was an only child. She'd gone to school at Conburrawong, before completing her final two years at boarding school in Brisbane.

That all seemed standard. If she'd decided she wanted to study medicine, moving to the city would have been sensible, and the elite boarding school she'd attended would have almost assured her a place in Brisbane's medical school.

While she was at university there'd been a series of part-time jobs, cleaning, washing dishes, standard student stuff which told him money had been short—maybe her parents had spent everything sending her to boarding school? But he'd seen nothing unusual. A brilliant undergraduate course, further training as a family doctor, then a series of placements.

It was only the placements that gave rise to questions. Until she'd moved to Kirra there'd been nothing longer than a year, and all of those had been part-time.

As was her present job. She was a part-time doctor, a part-time surf instructor. Also, he noted, there'd been no mention of her parents coming to the wedding.

Was she a loner like he was?

Why?

He glanced at her now and saw her face was set.

Was she afraid? Of what? The terms of the next two years had been spelt out clearly between them. This was a business contract, the only difference between this and any other contract being that it couldn't be put down on paper.

Was she afraid of him moving in with her? Afraid he'd intrude into her solitude?

'Jodie, you do know I'm not about to seduce you,' he ventured, and she swivelled to stare at him.

'What…?'

'You look afraid.'

'I'm not.' She took a deep breath. 'Of course I'm not. Besides, I know karate—and three other Japanese words.'

It was an attempt at a joke and it made him smile, but the tension was still there. She looked so wary.

How to break this moment? Give her space?

How? Go inside, head to separate bedrooms, close the doors and start their separate lives?

That was what they should do. In truth, the weariness that had followed since his last dose of dengue was weighing hard, but after such a day he knew sleep would be impossible.

So…

'So, given I'm dead scared of a karate-wielding woman—do you wield karate?—knowing you're absolutely safe, if I tell you I'm thinking I might head down to the beach for a swim, would you like to join me?'

'What, now?' she said, startled.

'Why not?'

She looked dubiously down towards the beach. The moonlight was glinting on the water, ripples of silver playing over the gentle surf. Surf? This wasn't a surf beach, it was more a wallow and paddle beach.

'Night feeders,' Jodie said.

'Night feeders?'

'I… Stingrays and stuff.'

'Really?'

'But…the water's so clear,' she murmured, and it was as if she was talking to herself. 'In this moonlight we could see everything.'

'And you know karate.'

And she smiled. It was a real smile too, tension easing. For a moment he let himself feel smug, but he had to keep going. He had to make her feel… safe?

Why would she not? It didn't make sense, but instinctively he knew to reinforce what he'd gained.

'Sadly, I don't know any karate,' he confessed. 'But I do want a swim so, if needs must, I'll go alone, with or without my warrior woman.' Then, 'Sorry. *A* warrior woman,' he amended, and to his relief she grinned.

'Okay then,' she told him. 'Let's go.'

CHAPTER EIGHT

THIS WAS THE strangest of nights, though surely no stranger than the day.

As Jodie struggled out of her dress she could hear Seb in the other room—his bedroom. Ditching his suit? He obviously didn't need to struggle with forty tiny buttons. Oh, the cost of being a fairy princess. But Seb's idea of a swim seemed a siren song. All she wanted right now was to be in her swimmers, for things to get back to normal.

But what was normal? Living with Seb?

Seb had moved his belongings into the cottage the night before, but he'd stayed at the resort until the ceremony. 'Because the islanders will expect it,' she'd told him. 'If we're going to do this, we need to do it right.'

But what would the islanders think of her resolution to not sleep with Seb at all? They'd think she was nuts, she acknowledged, or at least the island's women would. Seb was gorgeous any way you looked at it. Or looked at *him*. Why would she not want to sleep with him? What did the islanders really think of this strange wedding, of the publicity surrounding them?

Who cared? She certainly didn't—hadn't she gone through a lifetime of judgement and come out the other side? This arrangement made some sort of sense. Seb was to be a housemate and that was that. Except, right now, the bedroom wall seemed pretty thin.

And the noise next door had ceased. He was waiting for her.

A midnight swim. Was this crazy?

Oh, for heaven's sake, how many shared houses had she lived in, how many friends had she gone swimming with, at any time of the day?

The last button undone, her dress fell to the floor and she stepped out of it. She'd sell it online, she told herself. What a waste. Fancy pretending...

But she knew that she'd never have made it through this day without pretending. If she'd gone to a registry office, worn normal clothes, been who she really was, to make those vows would have been impossible.

So now I need to stop pretending, she told herself. *Now the reality is that I have a new housemate and we're going for a swim and then we're getting on with our lives.*

And that's all.

The fairy princess was gone. In her place was Jodie. His new housemate.

His wife.

Officially, the second title had to be front and centre, but personally, Jodie needed to be simply the woman who shared his house.

No. The woman who shared *her* house. This

needed to be on her terms, he told himself. So much depended on her holding it together.

Why did he think there was a risk that she couldn't?

Because he could sense her fear.

She emerged from the cottage, bridal gown and accessories gone, swimmers and towel in their place. She'd let her hair down and scraped off her make-up. She managed a smile, but he could tell it was forced.

'You lead the way,' he said gently, thinking she knew the path to the beach but there were so many other paths they'd need to negotiate.

Part of him wanted to reach out, to take her hand, to walk together in the moonlight, but he sensed enough not to even try. The silence between them seemed a tangible barrier, one they were almost afraid to break. So they walked in silence, reached the sand, dropped their towels and walked straight in.

The water was cool, deliciously so after the heat and tension of the day. They waded through the shallows without hesitation, then Seb dived into an oncoming wave. When he surfaced, Jodie was gone.

For a moment he was confused. He stood and looked—and found her surfacing further out. This woman was a seal, he thought, to stay under like that...

Did she want to swim alone? But surely she was too far out, and at this time of night...

Should he let her be?

She was treading water beyond the shallow breakers and she seemed almost to be waiting.

Was that wishful thinking? Regardless, the urge was suddenly overwhelming, to be in contact, to somehow make this night normal, to be...friends?

He dived under another wave, but this time he stayed under. He wasn't bad at swimming—he'd learned as a kid in the river near where his parents worked. He'd last swum on the day his great-uncle had had the accident, but his body knew what to do, even if physically that last dose of dengue had left its mark. He wasn't sure if his weakened lungs could manage to reach her, but he aimed at the place where Jodie was and stroked his body forward underwater until he ran out of air.

And when he surfaced, he was right before her. A metre, maybe even less.

He'd startled her. Even as he surfaced, he saw the shock, and he almost expected her to dive again. Instead, he saw the almost conscious decision to stay put.

'Scare a girl, why don't you?' she managed.

'Did you think I was a shark?'

'This beach is too shallow for sharks.'

'So what do you think I am?' he asked, and there was a question.

'My husband,' she said at last, flatly, without inflexion, and something in her voice made him wince.

'Is that so bad?'

'I... No.'

'Jodie, has someone hurt you?' It was shallow enough here for them to be able to stand—just. They could relax enough to talk, but there was nothing relaxed about the way she was looking at him. He was starting to think...abusive relationship in the past? Violence? It fitted with the fear.

'No,' she said flatly.

He didn't believe her. Somewhere in her past, someone had hurt this woman, badly.

'I will never do anything you don't like,' he said, but thought: *That sounds weak...there must be a better way of saying it. How do you reassure a woman who's experienced...what?*

'You'd better not,' she muttered.

'Because of karate?' He smiled and hoped she'd smile back. Their eyes locked. There was a moment's stillness—and then finally she did smile. And there was even a trace of relief.

'Because of karate,' she agreed. 'Seb, believe it or not, I do trust you.'

'That's a relief,' he said, wondering if he did believe it. He thought about probing more but the tension had lessened and he wanted to keep it that way. 'Okay, how about we race to the end of the cove?'

'I'd beat you.'

'I'd like to see you try!'

She did beat him and she felt a bit astonished.

She was a strong swimmer but speed wasn't her strength. She could surf for hours, she could fight her way through breakers twice her height, but she'd learned long ago that when it came to sprints most decent male swimmers could beat her.

And Seb did, for half the distance, but then, just as she was feeling as if she was falling back, she sensed rather than saw him slacken.

A bit puzzled, she slowed her own pace, hopefully not so much that he'd notice, but honestly, did she really want to beat the pants off him on her wedding night? Guys have pride, she thought, maybe a bit condescendingly, but most women would understand the instinct to nobly grant him a win. It was dumb, but did it matter?

And practically, he should win. His almost naked body in the moonlight had looked lean and muscled. Seeing him dressed only in board-shorts, she'd felt…well, possibly not what it was wise to feel, given her vow to stay apart. But when he'd dropped the towel he'd had draped around his shoulders, she'd been aware of a jolt that was purely primeval.

Down, girl, she'd told herself. That sort of hormonal urge meant trouble and she wasn't going there. But she had been expecting him to beat her.

Hoping that he'd at least match her? Why was it important to her that he was strong?

Well, that's primeval too, she'd told herself as she slowed. *Human, animal, whatever, as in nature, the fastest, fittest, strongest gets the girl.*

'Except this girl isn't to be got,' she muttered under her breath, and as they neared the rocks that bordered the cove's end she put on a spurt of speed that meant she did beat him.

She reached the edge of the cove and surfaced by the rock ledge, then watched him come in behind her. He finished, found his feet and waited for a moment, breathing heavily.

'Okay, I'm out of practice,' he managed. 'So I now have two years to get fit.'

But he looked spent, she thought, and suddenly the medical side of her kicked in. She let him recover for a moment and then ventured, 'Seb, you copped dengue three times?'

'Yeah, the last knocked the stuffing out of me,' he admitted, obviously realising what she was on about.

'And the third bout was eighteen months ago?'

'Hey, isn't this our wedding night? Can I make an appointment to see you professionally in the morning?' Then he sighed and relented. 'Okay. Yes, it was eighteen months ago and I still have some fatigue.'

'And yet you're challenging me to race when you've already had a huge day.'

'Moving on,' he said firmly. 'I'm fine.'

'Except puffed. Physician heal thyself?' she quoted.

'There's nothing any other physician can do. I just need time.'

Okay, she conceded. He was probably right. On-going fatigue could be a long-term side-effect of dengue, and tonight was hardly the time to talk medicine.

'We'll get you fit,' she told him. 'Two years on the island… A swim every day… A bit of surfing…'

'There'll hardly be time. I still need to work.'

'Of course you do. But you also need to relax.'

'Yes, Mum,' he said, and she raised her hand and splashed him. It was a practised move and a wall of water hit him full-on. He gasped and choked, and when his eyes cleared, she saw disbelief—and then challenge.

'Haven't we talked about expectations within this marriage?' he demanded, and she blinked.

'What?'

'Surely we should have included this. Love, honour and obey—and don't splash!'

'There was *not* an obey.'

'Really? There must have been respect at least. I was too discombobulated by the princess bride bit. Which was gorgeous, by the way. But did we get a copy of our vows? What the hell have we signed?'

'You signed a pledge to give me a million dollars. I remember that.'

'That was the legal bit, not included in the wedding vows. And even if it was…a million doesn't include splashing your husband.'

And, for answer, she raised her hand and splashed again.

'Pooh,' she said.

It was like a battle cry. Pooh? How was a man to ignore such a taunt. Almost instinctively, he raised his own hand and splashed back.

And kept right on splashing.

They'd been concerned—a little—about night feeders. There was no such worry now. No matter what sea creatures were lurking in the depths, the furious splashing that ensued would surely have sent any self-respecting critter to the depths. For it didn't stop. Suddenly, it felt like all the tension of the day, maybe all the tension of the last month, found itself a way to explode. A man and a woman, standing breast deep in the surf, splashing like their lives depended on it.

It was almost as if the spray of water was holding each of them at a distance that seemed vital. It was ridiculous, childlike, starting almost as a joke but somehow turning to something serious. Was there anger there, frustration, fear?

Or was that just her? Jodie thought. What was she doing, splashing this man as if her life depended on somehow holding him at bay? She splashed and splashed and then, when finally he ceased, she hardly noticed.

Until his hand came out and caught her arm.

'Jodie,' he said very softly as she tried to splash again with her free arm. 'Jodie, I've promised I won't hurt you. I've promised I'll respect your independence. What's wrong?'

'I... Nothing's wrong.'

'Then why are you so scared?'

'And why are you so tired?' she countered. It didn't make sense as a retort but it was all she had. She tugged back against his hold but he didn't release it.

'I told you. I'm still recovering from dengue,' he replied, softly though, as if gentleness could reassure her. Really? Gentleness was the way to get under her defences. She didn't need it. She didn't! 'So will you tell me what you're recovering from?'

'I'm not.'

'No?'

'It's none of your business.'

'I know it's not.' They stood silently for a moment, both of them looking down at the link, his hand on her arm. And then slowly, carefully, he released it, but instead of stepping away he lifted his hand. He touched her cheek and then, so lightly, he traced her cheekbone. Almost as if he was searching for tears, which was crazy, seeing as her face was dripping with seawater.

But did he know how close to tears she was? Why on earth? What was she doing, wanting to cry?

It was the day, she told herself frantically. The emotion. The build-up and the tension.

The fear.

What did she have to be afraid of? she asked herself with something akin to desperation. This was a contract only. It meant nothing. How could it mean anything?

He let his fingers drop but he didn't move back. 'You're safe, Jodie,' he said softly. 'I swear.'

And, as if on cue, something brushed her leg.

What was it? Seaweed? No, something solid. Moving!

To say she levitated would not be an understatement. Somehow, some way, she was in the air—and when she descended, she was in Seb's arms. And he had her and he was lifting her away, striding back out of the waves into the shallows.

Chuckling?

Chuckling!

'What…? What…?' The shock of something brushing her leg wasn't as great as being in this man's arms.

'It looked like a groper,' he told her. 'A big 'un. I saw its shadow in the moonlight. It bumped right into you. I've never seen a woman levitate before.'

'A groper…' She caught her breath. Of course. She'd seen one here before, a big, beautiful creature that moseyed around in the shallows.

Gropers were a lot more wary of humans than humans were of them, and given noise and splashing, they'd flee. It had probably been hiding under the rock ledge, and then, when the splashing got too close, decided the safest course was to get out and bolt.

They were harmless. There'd been no reason at all for her to end up in this guy's arms, and for him to be carrying her out of the water.

'I... Put me down,' she said shakily.

'When I reach the sand,' he promised. 'Chivalry demands no less.'

'Seb...'

'You can't expect to do the fairy princess bit and not have a gallant knight do his thing in return,' he said severely. 'Where's my sword when I need it? Or my pet dragon?'

And then, to her own astonishment, she heard herself giggle. Giggle! She was being carried, whether she liked it or not. She was in this guy's arms and...

And why not enjoy it?

She was being carried by her husband. The thought should have been overwhelming, it should have been enough for her to fight to be put down, to retreat to the place where she always retreated, her own head, her only place of refuge.

But oh, the way she was starting to feel. This was crazy, but somehow a tiny betraying sliver of her brain was saying, *You've dated before. You've had fun before. Why is this any different? You can surely enjoy this man, enjoy his body, take pleasure and walk away, as you've walked away in the past?*

The logical part of her brain was trying to yell a response—*No! You can't walk away. You'll be living with this guy for two years, like it or not. Don't be so stupid. What you need are barriers, so put them up now!*

But that betraying sliver was growing louder. *You've walked away before, no problems. You can do it again. Just for tonight... Just for now...*

He'd reached the shore but, instead of putting her down, he carried her further up the beach, to where they'd dumped their towels.

'There'll be crabs,' he told her before she'd even protested. 'I've already saved you from a groper, and I'm on a roll. A knight in shining armour. If I've saved you this far, I'm not about to let you get nibbled by sand crabs.'

And astonishingly she heard herself giggle again, and that betraying voice turned into a betraying clamour that was almost enveloping her whole brain. A knight in shining armour... How crazy was that, but this night...this man...this moment...

What was happening? She had no idea. All she knew was that something weird was taking over. This whole fantasy, this night, the moonlight on the water, this man's arms...

And when finally he reached the pile of towels and set her back on her feet, the fantasy held. She found she'd lost all capacity to step back, to move away.

And he didn't move back either. His hands were still resting lightly on her waist. He was smiling down at her, his gaze gentle and a little quizzical.

'Safe, Jodie love?' he said softly.

'I… Yes. Thank you for saving me from…a groper.'

'It's my very great pleasure,' he told her, and she looked up at him and saw his smile—and something inside her simply melted.

This wasn't what was supposed to happen. She wasn't allowed to feel like this. No!

But why not? What was she scared of?

Was she scared?

Somewhere, under the woman fighting an inner battle right now, was the Jodie who lived life on her terms. Who'd made decisions years back to call the shots. Who'd had the stuffing kicked out of her at fifteen—or even earlier, if she was honest—who'd had to live with the anger and emptiness caused by the decisions of others and had resolved never again to do…what was expected. What was demanded.

What was demanded, right now, was that she keep her distance.

The sensible voice in her head—the one she'd trained for years—was shouting, *Stay away from*

this guy, don't let him near, keep your distance.
But this night, this fantasy, this man, they were
all conspiring to allow another voice to build. The
voice that said, *You know you want to. Who's to
say you can't?*

No one.

Be sensible, the first voice whispered, but it was
struggling to be heard. The second was drown-
ing it out. Because of this night? Because of this
man? Because of the way he'd carried her out of
the surf, because of the way he was looking at her,
smiling at her…respecting her wishes?

So many sensations had been building over
these past weeks. The images of him in Al Delebe, doing such good. Seb, a man of such power,
looking at her shabby little cottage and not rais-
ing any doubts. Yes, he'd live here, yes, he'd do
what he could, but she knew it wasn't just for him.
There was so much at stake, so much he could do
for so many.

He was so…so Seb? Her mind couldn't find the
right descriptors, but she must. She was fighting
for logic but it was nowhere. After all the logic
she'd used to agree to this arrangement, was her
body suddenly deciding to capitulate?

Capitulate? It was no such thing, her inner voice
was saying. She was taking power back, because
right now she wanted him.

She'd had lovers before, of course she had—that
disastrous adolescent fumble hadn't put her off for

ever. Boyfriends had been transient, no strings attached. She'd enjoyed them. Sometimes she'd even fancied she'd loved them, but she'd always moved on. So why not this man?

Why not take this night, this time, even these two years and milk it for all it was worth? Why not…?

He was looking down at her, still smiling, but the smile was gently questioning. Seb. This man.

And in the face of that smile, the inner voices faded to nothing. The arguments were a muddled mess, to be kicked aside in the face of something far, far more important.

Before she knew what her betraying self intended, she raised herself on her toes, she looped her hands around his neck—and she kissed him.

And as her mouth met his, as his arms strengthened their hold, as her tentative kiss was met with a desire that said he felt the same, the last of her qualms dissolved.

She was being held close, cradled, skin against skin, wet, warm, filled with adrenaline, high from the day…

Wanting.

The voices could go fight among themselves, she thought with the last sliver of consciousness available for such awareness. This man, this night, this moment—this was all that mattered.

The fear could take itself right out to sea and disappear for ever.

* * *

One moment he was swimming with a woman who seemed almost afraid to look at him. A woman—*his wife*—who'd seemed nothing but clinical and businesslike as she'd organised a wedding that was pure fantasy, and then who'd stepped out of her fantasy clothes and moved on. She was a bride under contract for two years, a paid arrangement, a million dollars for a make-believe bride.

And then there'd been one groper, brushing a leg, causing her to jump, causing him to catch her in his arms, causing him to feel the warmth, the strength of her body, causing...desire.

But maybe there'd always been desire. He had to admit it. The first time he'd seen her, working professionally, a competent, brisk doctor, tired and frustrated with both him and his arrogant great-uncle, there'd been a frisson of something he'd struggled to understand.

Or maybe he did understand it. Maybe it was a feeling as old as time itself.

This was a no-frills woman, normally in shorts and T-shirt, now in a sliver of a bikini, with nothing to hide her essential essence. A woman who said what she thought. A woman who...

Who...what? He didn't know. He hardly knew her at all, he conceded, but he knew her enough to realise there were barriers that meant she kept herself to herself—that this wedding was purely business.

And this day, this wedding, had cemented that. Yes, they'd made vows, but he had enough intuition to sense that it wasn't Jodie making the vows. It was a front, a carefully orchestrated defence, a way of keeping herself apart.

But now... One sea creature brushing her leg...

No. It was more than that, much more. The culmination of what?

The straw that broke the camel's back? The analogy drifted across his thoughts. Was that what it was? A slow build of desire that culminated in this?

It was surely like that for him—only this was no straw. He too had built barriers—he'd had to. All his life, there'd been so much need. Even as a kid he'd had it instilled into him. *You can do good, Seb. We can do good.* But most of that good had been done by holding himself apart. Not needing his parents. Taking a back seat to their desire to do good.

He remembered getting appendicitis as a child, when his parents were about to leave on field work. He'd been handed over to another doctor on the team. 'Aaden will look after you, mate. We'll radio in tonight to see how you are, but you'll be fine.'

There'd been weird Christmases, carefully orchestrated, always in Al Delebe, where he'd been showered with gifts from his parents, so many gifts. And then, after a morning playing feverishly because he knew what would happen, there'd always been a serious talk with his parents. They'd used his over-the-top Christmas as a teaching tool.

'Seb, you have so much, and there are so many kids in the camp here, sitting with nothing while their parents wait for treatment. But it's your decision...'

Was it really his decision? Maybe it had been, but in the process, he'd learned about things being taken away.

Even his parents. He remembered one of the doctors in Al Delebe talking to him after his parents' death. 'You must be proud, Seb. They gave their all.'

So he got it, Jodie's barriers. They were rational, expected, to be encouraged. This fantasy wedding had been sensible. The plans for living with her, the organisation of his life, they too made sense.

This swim, though, had been a bad idea, fatigue, the emotions of the day leaving them open to...

Open to his bride being in his arms, him carrying her out of the water, feeling the warmth, the delicious curving of her body against his wet chest, the way she'd shuddered and then clung. The way he'd set her down and she'd looked up at him. The straw that broke the camel's back? The chink in both of their armour.

But, armour or not, it no longer mattered—it could no longer matter. For now, their defences had dissolved. She'd looked at him for that long, considering moment—and then she'd smiled and raised herself to meet his kiss.

And then there was only this night. This moment. This woman.

The kiss… Its power…

He was lost.

Or maybe he wasn't lost. Maybe this was where he was meant to be. This perfect place, this wonderful woman. His bride.

And for a moment he let himself think, he let himself believe…

Had he learned nothing? All those Christmases…

But they were in the past, gone. Here, there was only Jodie, the feel of her, the taste, the way she was moulding to his body, her breasts against his chest, her arms holding him, claiming…her man?

His bride.

This was no fantasy bride, he thought as he held her close, as he savoured the feel and taste of her, as the last of those damned defences crumbled to nothing. The glorious golden vision of a bride who'd made vows beside him this day had been unreal and of no account. This was the real Jodie in his arms right now.

This was…his true bride?

CHAPTER NINE

THEY WOKE SPOONED against each other in Jodie's big bed. There'd been no choice between rooms. Seb had furnished his with a single bed so he could fit a desk and filing cabinets into the room, setting it up so he could continue life as he knew it.

Only somehow life had changed.

It had been a real wedding night. Somehow, they'd made it home, laughing, stumbling, holding each other, but each sure of what lay ahead.

'Jodie, do you really…?' he remembered asking. He'd had to ask, but as they'd reached the house she'd turned within his hold and kissed him again, long, languorous, the heat within building to unbearable limits.

'I'm no virgin bride, Seb Cantrell,' she'd breathed. 'Rational or not, right now, I want you and I know what I'm doing. So…you?'

There'd been no need for him to answer, and now he lay with Jodie spooned against his chest, skin against skin. He could feel her heartbeat. He could almost taste the salt of her. Wisps of her hair were lying across his shoulders and he felt…

She stirred and suddenly he was remembering those Christmases. The memories were dumb, outdated, something to be forgotten, but instinctively his arm tightened around her.

To have and to hold... That had been in the wedding vows, surely. For two glorious years... to have and to hold.

Her eyes were open. She twisted within his hold and she was gazing at him with an expression he couldn't hope to understand.

'You look like the cat that got the cream,' she whispered, and he smiled and she smiled back.

'So do you,' he told her. 'Mutual bliss?'

'Yep.' She stirred and stretched, a movement so sensual that he had to fight to stop himself pulling her back in to him. There were things that needed to be said. Surely there were.

Oh, but he wanted her.

'Jodie...'

'Yeah, I know,' she whispered. 'Barriers. This wasn't supposed to happen, but there's no law against it, is there? To have fun?'

'Every night for the next two years?' he managed, and she raised herself on one elbow and gazed down at him.

'One night at a time,' she murmured and then seemed to force herself back to reality. He could see her face tighten.

'Seb, it can't be a real marriage.'

'Yeah, we're playing with fire,' he managed. 'An affair where we're held together for two years... What about things like...well, snoring?'

'Did I snore?' She sat up promptly and gazed down at him in shock. 'Did I?'

'No, but you might have. And so might I. Or we might discover we have different toothpaste-squeezing techniques. I've heard that's driven thousands of couples apart.'

'Seb, we're not a couple.'

'No,' he agreed cautiously. Where was this going? He had no idea. Married and yet not? Where was the rulebook? But then he said, almost before he could help himself, 'Jodie, is there any reason we can't be?'

'No. No!'

'Because?'

'Because I don't know you.'

'Fair enough.' He lifted his hand and traced her cheekbone with his finger—and saw her shudder. There was trouble in her eyes, but he also saw the flash of desire. All he wanted right now was to take her in his arms again, to sink back into the wonders of the night before, but there were boundaries that obviously needed to be adjusted.

'I'm a loner,' Jodie said, and he nodded.

'I can see that. So am I. We have no need to share toothpaste. But can two loners manage to have fun as well as get on with their lone lives? Lone when we need to be, together when we don't.'

'How can that possibly work?'

'I have no idea,' he told her. 'But maybe we could try. And if it did end up that we wanted…'

'Seb, I won't have kids.'

There was a bald statement, seemingly coming

from nowhere, and it shocked them both. The silence stretched on. Jodie lay down again, but this time she wasn't touching him. They lay looking upward, thinking...what?

'Jodie, if we wanted to have kids, I'd need to ask you to marry me,' he said at last.

'You already have.' It was a whisper and she sounded...scared.

'No. My great-uncle did. He coerced both of us into this situation.' He took a breath, trying to think it through. 'He was trying to change both our lives, and maybe he's done it. But it was coercion, blackmail if you like, and we don't have to agree to blackmail.'

She hesitated and then said, almost reluctantly, 'I guess it was blackmail.'

'So we don't need to play his game. Yes, we've married, sort of. Yes, we've ended up in bed, which is probably what he intended. But the rest...'

'He wants us to have kids.'

'Wanted. Past tense.' Her body was still touching him, but only just. A sliver of skin against his hip. Warm to touch. Enough to make a man want...'

But he had to take this slowly. Last night had been a time out of frame—part of the fantasy. Right now, he was in bed with a woman he sensed wanted to run.

'Where we go from here has nothing to do with my uncle,' he said at last, feeling his way with

care. 'He doesn't control us. Last night…this…
it felt…it feels like something we both want, not
something he orchestrated. Is that right? You don't
feel coerced?'

'Um…no,' she conceded, and he even heard the
trace of a smile in her voice. 'Or, if I'm honest,
maybe I even did the coercing.'

'Mutual coercing,' he said and grinned, and he
felt himself relax a little. 'And that's the way it
needs to be. Checking along the way to see if we're
pushing boundaries. Honestly, one day I might
want kids.' Did he? He'd never imagined himself
with children. Why was he thinking of them now?
'But that's a whole future consideration,' he said
hastily. 'With you or someone else. That's not part
of our deal.'

'It had better not be.'

He frowned then and it was his turn to prop
himself on one elbow and look down at her. The
tone of her voice… 'Jodie, what is there in that
to make you afraid? As if you think somehow I
could persuade…'

'You couldn't.'

'I know I couldn't.' He didn't get this. Here was
a vibrant, strong woman, accepting this situation
on her own terms, and yet reacting with what
seemed like panic. 'Jodie, is it the idea of kids
that makes you frightened?'

'I'm not frightened.'

'Maybe that's the wrong word.' He was looking

into her eyes and he was still sensing panic. 'But you're alone, and you seem always to be alone. I've asked you before... Has some guy hurt you in the past? Some lowlife?'

'No.'

'Really?'

'Leave it, Seb,' she said. 'My past is my business. If we were really married...'

'Even then I wouldn't push.'

'Good.' She closed her eyes for a moment—and when she opened them he saw the fear had been replaced by determination.

'Okay, moving on.' She rolled sideways and rose, standing for a moment, naked, beautiful, smiling down at him with a wry smile. He noticed a scratch running down the back of her leg but before he could say anything she'd grabbed a robe. 'Enough of the intense discussion, Seb. I'm hungry. Toast and coffee?'

'Let me make them.'

'Nope.' She shook her head, her lovely hair swinging out behind her. 'I need a shower and then I need toast and Vegemite and time sitting on the porch saying good morning to the morning. Separate breakfasts, Dr Cantrell. Separate lives.'

'So what about tonight?'

Dear heaven, she was beautiful. Breathtaking. It was all he could do not to reach out for her again.

'We'll let tonight take care of itself,' she said, her serene and confident façade in place again.

'But what happens under bedclothes stays between bedclothes. Our real lives are different.'

Did that mean...? There was a leap of hope.

But she was backing away, still smiling. 'I might or might not invite you to my bed again,' she said. 'Okay, based on last night's performance, the likelihood of it happening is pretty strong. But that's it.'

'And if I invite you to mine?'

'Every invite will be considered on its merits,' she said demurely, and then she grinned, once again a woman in charge of her world. 'There are no promises, Seb Cantrell, but I don't see why parts of your Uncle Arthur's crazy last will and testament shouldn't turn out to be...fun.'

She showered, standing under cold water, closing her eyes, blocking the noise of the last twenty-four hours from her mind, deliberately putting her mind into neutral. But neutral refused to happen.

She tugged on shorts and T-shirt, she carried her toast and coffee outside, sat on the front steps and considered her day, acutely aware that Seb was still in the cottage behind her.

Still in her bed?

What had just happened?

So much for separate living, she thought ruefully. It would have been fine if her new husband wasn't so gorgeous. If he wasn't so sexy.

If he hadn't made her feel like the most desirable woman he'd ever held.

Maybe he did that with all his women, she thought. With all his wives? The idea made her smile a little, but there was trouble behind the smile.

She hadn't meant this to happen, and to feel like this on the day after her mock wedding... It went against everything she'd ever promised herself.

And kids...

Where had that discussion come from? Why had they even talked about it?

Because she'd brought it up, she conceded, and once aired it had hung. A possibility.

Not a possibility. Oh, the pain...

She was playing with fire here, opening herself up to hurt, betrayal...

She was doing no such thing. She was still in control, she told herself fiercely. She could still call the shots.

But should calling the shots mean allowing Seb to keep holding her as he'd held her last night? Could it mean allowing herself to love him back?

Love? Where had that word come from? She'd meant hold. But even hold... To continue to hold him... It really was playing with fire.

But how could she not? The feel of him, the taste, the touch... The way her body responded to his. The feeling that...here was her home.

Well, that was crazy, she told herself angrily. She was a loner and she intended staying that way.

But, as if on cue, the screen door opened and banged shut again. Seb came out, carrying coffee. The veranda steps were wide and he sat just about as far away from her as he could—but he was still sitting on *her* step.

Go away. That was what she wanted to say, but she couldn't quite form the words. Which was just as well, she told herself. It'd be petty. What was more, it'd smack of fear—and who was afraid?

Why on earth should she be afraid?

And then a car pulled into the drive and Angus and Misty and the kids piled out, smiling and laughing. Their little boy was still wearing his Space Stars costume from the wedding. Forrest had been one of the leading kids in the pageboy procession. There'd probably be island kids wearing crazy costumes for months.

'Good morning,' Misty called, at eight months pregnant struggling to get out of the car. 'Congratulations, newlyweds. We have your gift.'

'Our gift?' Jodie rose, feeling thoroughly discombobulated. This scene was far too domestic. Too…close? And then she forgot about being discombobulated—or maybe discombobulation went up a notch, because Forrest was reaching back into the car and lifting out…a puppy.

'So how was the wedding night?' Angus, the island's senior doctor, was grinning broadly as he looked at the two of them. 'You want to tell us about it?' And then he shook his head. 'Okay, don't answer that, we don't want to know.'

'Yes, we do,' his wife retorted. 'Any details you want to share, Jodie, love, we're all ears.'

'In front of the children?' Angus grinned as he tried to frown her down, but by then all attention was on the puppy.

He—she?—was beautiful. Adorable. Chocolate-box cute.

A golden retriever? Maybe not, because there was a hint of something else, maybe a collie? The island wasn't known for pedigree dogs. Regardless, the pup was fluffy and golden, with huge brown eyes that were gazing out at the world with awe, and a tail that was rotating like a helicopter blade. Forrest was struggling to contain the bundle of wriggling excitement.

'Seb, this is Forrest,' Jodie said, introducing Seb to the kid holding the pup. She added, very, very cautiously, 'And who's this? I didn't know you guys were getting a puppy.'

'We're not,' Forrest said happily. 'This is yours.'

'Ours?' Why did something inside her feel as if it was freezing?

But Misty's smile was pure mischief. 'I know, you don't want commitment, but this is our wedding gift.' Then, as Jodie stared in stunned silence, she continued, almost as if this was no big deal, 'Well, we had to give you something. Our best friend and colleague getting married is a really big deal. When we got our Biggles you said you still didn't know how long you were staying, and you couldn't commit to a puppy. That meant you missed out on Biggles's sister or brother, which made us sad because we know how much you love him. Every time you come to our place, he's all over you. But now...'

She paused, grinning, looking from Jodie to Seb and back again. 'Well, you've told us the terms of your marriage. We understand it's a fixed term contract. We get it.' There was another pause then, while she seemed to focus attention on Seb's hand—still on Jodie's arm—but she forged on. 'So okay, it's only for two years, but why should you miss out on so much because your time's limited? We think Biggles and Freya...this is Freya, by the way...are bound to get on. Therefore...'

She paused again, as if gathering her words, but then continued on a note of triumph, 'So, at the end of two years, if you really both decide to walk away, if you haven't fallen in love—with Freya, I mean,' she added hastily, 'no pressure on you two, then we'll take her back. But she's from a Craig McConachie litter, which means there's a queue if you really don't want her. So, say so now and we'll give you, I don't know, a frying pan or a set of towels instead.' She paused and looked hopefully from Jodie to Seb and then back again. 'So, what do you say?'

A dog. Commitment. Emotion. No. Her heart screamed it. *No!*

But Seb had dropped her arm and was already moving forward. Forrest lifted the pup to meet him and Seb gathered the pup into his arms. And as he cradled the fluffy golden package Jodie felt…lost.

What had Misty said? *'If you haven't fallen in love…'*

She'd meant with the dog.

She didn't do love. She didn't love…anything.

But Seb was holding the pup—Freya. Freya was trying her best to lick every part of Seb's face she could possibly reach, and Jodie's friends were laughing and the look on Seb's face…

He was standing in the early morning sunlight, wearing faded jeans and T-shirt and nothing else. His dark hair was wet from the shower, his feet were bare, he stood wrangling his armful of ecstatic pup—and his face said… Love?

And with a moment's flash of intuition, she knew this was the perfect gift. She knew he'd fallen in love.

How could he fall like this? How could he?

Why could she not?

Because…

'You're not allergic, are you?' It was Forrest, nine years old and obviously worried about the way she was reacting. 'Miriam at school is allergic. She wanted a dog and she had to get a poodle.'

'She can't be allergic,' Misty told him. 'Have

you seen the way she cuddles Biggles, and Biggles is an allergenic dog. Very allergenic,' she added darkly. 'You should see our sofa.'

'But do you want her?' Forrest asked, still looking worried.

And then, suddenly, all eyes were on her.

Everyone present knew that Seb was sold. He was still holding the pup, still trying to calm her down, but now he was watching her as well, his dark eyes questioning.

'Jodie, if you don't want her...' he said, suddenly talking only to her. 'She'll be a lot of work, Jodie, love, and I'll be in Brisbane three days a week. I think it needs to be up to you.'

And he got it, she thought. It was unspoken but it was in his voice, in his look. There was an understanding...

Or maybe not an understanding. He didn't know—how could he—the pain that was always in her heart. None of these people knew the pain of loss.

This was a dog. Not a child. A dog!

Why did it feel so terrifying? As if she was facing a chasm and if she took one step forward...

And he'd called her *Jodie, love*'...

'Jodie?' Seb asked gently. He stepped towards her, still carrying the pup. For a moment she thought he was going to put it into her arms and she took an instinctive step back.

Everyone else was silent, not understanding but somehow…surely sensing how big a deal this was.

And then Seb put the pup down. 'Jodie, I won't do anything you don't want,' he reiterated. 'None of us will. I would love the pup—I can't disguise it. If at the end of two years you don't want her to stay here, then she can come with me back to the mainland. I think… Well, for some reason, things seem to be changing for me, all sorts of things, and maybe I need to make room for…other things in my life. And it seems Freya is one of them. So, once again, no commitment after two years, but if you want her for now…'

'I'll fall for her,' she whispered.

'I already have,' Seb said, speaking to her only. 'It's a leap into the unknown, but what's life if not a succession of leaps?'

And…he got it, she thought. He understood her fear.

How?

There was no way of knowing. All she knew was that she had a choice: back away…or leap.

And the pup was sniffing and waddling forward, finding her bare toes, giving them an investigative lick. Then she looked up, her big eyes seeming to implore, her tail wagging with hope.

Oh, for heaven's sake, what was there to fear in one pup? What?

And while her friends watched on, while Seb smiled his smile, questioning but somehow understanding, finally, she reached down and scooped her up.

And as her arms closed on the warm, wriggling mass she thought—*Why does this seem more real—why does this seem more terrifying—than the vows I made last night?*

The feeling he'd had when he'd lifted the pup into his arms was almost indescribable.

All his life he'd been a loner. He'd been loved, though—of course he had—but... His parents had been passionate about their work, so passionate that his arrival had been a mistake. Once his mother had even said, 'We couldn't justify bringing someone else into the world when there's so much to be done.'

Once he was there though, they'd loved him to the best of their ability, but he'd had to fit into their world. He was minded by others as they'd worked. As he'd grown into someone who could be useful he'd been trained to help, but he'd been sent back to Australia to boarding school as soon as his health had interfered with their work.

For his parents, the idea of stopping, of spending time, what, smelling the roses, was anathema to them. As was the thought of doing something so useless as owning a dog.

Or loving a woman who couldn't advance his work?

Where had that thought come from? But it was

there as he watched Jodie lift the puppy into her arms, as he watched the fear on her face, as he watched her expression almost crumple as Freya's wriggles seemed to transform into ecstasy.

This woman...

He didn't know her. She was a woman his parents would have castigated as wasting her time, not using her talents, not committing herself to the greater good. Part-time medicine. Surfing. Lying in the sun and almost aggressively batting away connection.

But there were reasons. He knew it.

He thought of the night that had just gone, the passion, the fierceness of her lovemaking. The aching desire...

What was driving her? What?

He had two years to find out.

What was he thinking? Of making this...permanent?

Why not? If he could persuade her to commit to his passions? If he could persuade her to care?

To care for him—or to care for the whole world?

Maybe she couldn't do one without the other. But if she was onside... He had a sudden flash of his parents, facing down obstacle after obstacle, fighting together for what they both believed in. With Jodie by his side...

It was too soon. Somehow, he'd need to expose the shadows in her past, somehow get past the rigid control that seemed to be holding her in thrall.

To make her part of his world?

It was far too soon, he told himself firmly, but as he watched her hold the pup—were there tears tracking down her face?—he thought, *Why not?*

And then he thought of all those Christmases past, gifts given and then taken away.

Was this something that would be taken away? Were his fears somehow shared by Jodie?

He didn't understand, but this pup was theirs, he thought. It was a shared gift, and maybe together they could fight for it. Even when this time on the island was over, they could surely fit a dog into a life of doing good. Maybe there was some way this could work.

His conscience needn't even bother him. These two years were set aside to build for the future.

And in two years, maybe he might even persuade Jodie to be part of that future.

CHAPTER TEN

He worked too hard.

They'd been married for three months and in all that time she'd persuaded him to take three whole days off.

One had been for Isabelle Grundy's funeral— an all-island affair, seeing the old lady out in style. One had been when Misty and Angus had introduced their newest addition to the island, a tiny girl named Alice. That had involved a naming ceremony and then a party—music, laughter and far too much food.

In the face of such joy, Seb and Jodie had danced into the night, inhibitions, cares forgotten, but that had led to the third day off. Seb's stomach had cramped during the night, he'd woken whey-faced, and Jodie had almost had to barricade him into the room to keep him in bed.

He wasn't well. There was nothing specific, but living in the same house with him, sharing meals, sensing his slight withdrawal and the way his face sometimes seemed to close... If he was her patient, she'd have packed him off to Brisbane to see a specialist physician, but he wasn't her patient.

If he'd simply been a patient she might not have seen any signs to worry her, but sharing her house—okay, sharing her bed—she was aware that things weren't right.

He'd been extraordinarily lucky to survive three bouts of dengue fever. She knew that, and she also accepted that long-term fatigue was almost to be expected. But at times he seemed…ill. He was careful with what he ate, almost to the point of hunger. There were times when he hurt. In a patient she might not have picked up the subtle signs. She might have accepted fatigue as a reason, but living with him, holding him…

Worrying about him?

'I've pretty much taken care of myself for over thirty years now,' he growled when she tried to voice her niggles. And then he'd added, as he'd seen her real concern, 'Jodie, the last bout of dengue hit me hard and I was warned recovery could take years. So, this is normal. It can be a nuisance—symptoms come and go, usually when they're least wanted. The way I see it, though, is that I can ignore it and get on with my life, or I can treat myself as an invalid until such time as my body decides to cooperate. Which, Professor Martin, head of tropical diseases at the North Queensland Institute, tells me would do more harm than good. I have regular blood tests, I'm monitored and I'm as good as can be expected.'

'So you have seen him,' she said, worry backing off a little.

'I'm all grown up,' he told her, and then, seeing the cloud of concern in her eyes, he'd taken her face in his hands and kissed her. 'I don't take risks with my health. But I love you for worrying.'

And that word—love—it did make her back off. She didn't know what to do with it.

They were now solidly established in the routine they'd set themselves. Seb worked three days a week in Brisbane but he took the ferry home each night. Jodie was working as she normally did, in the clinic on the island, doing house calls, surfing when she could, playing with Freya. Trying not to feel like she was constantly waiting for Seb to come home. Trying to tell herself she wasn't doing any such thing.

But even when he was home he was working, at his desk, on the phone, constantly driving himself. Sometimes he had to take extra days in Brisbane, spending time at Cantrell Holdings, struggling to understand a business he wanted to change.

He worked and worked—and stayed apart.

Except at night. At night they shared her bed and she loved it.

And that was fine, she told herself, trying to justify her pleasure in lovemaking that was possibly more than a little stupid in what was little more than a short-term arrangement. But the temptation was irresistible—to enjoy each other's bodies under the sheets, and during the daylight hours to be apart.

But, more and more, it seemed boundaries were being crossed.

But what boundaries? They were hazy, she conceded. Ill-defined. The two-year boundary was the only thing that had persuaded her into this situation, but Seb always seemed to be overstepping her admittedly indistinct limits. Like when she'd worried out loud about his health. He'd reassured her and then he'd kissed her, in broad daylight, in the kitchen, which was supposed to be neutral territory. And then he'd scooped up Freya—already a lanky juvenile—and hugged the pup. Like he wanted to hug her?

He'd used the word *love*.

It was worrying because he seemed to be savouring this situation. When he arrived back after being in Brisbane, he'd hug Freya, and increasingly he hugged her. Until she backed off. Which was probably stupid, but she was struggling with boundaries she hardly knew herself.

More and more, she thought Seb was acting like…he was hungry for family? It was a family, though, that only existed in the fragments of time he had left in his crazy schedule. He didn't want more.

He seemed to want a family, but only on his terms.

Well, maybe that was like her own family, she told herself. That construct had been on her parents' terms, a family to be wiped as soon as the rules were broken.

This one was to be wiped at the end of two years.

But still, as the months rolled on, as their lives

settled into a routine she could deal with, she found herself relaxing a little. Housemates with benefits? That seemed okay. If she could keep her boundaries almost intact, well, the benefits were obvious. The way he made her body feel... The way he smiled at her and kissed her as they woke... The way he went out onto the veranda and stretched and seemed to soak in the sounds of the dawn chorus before another frantic day... The way he frowned over his laptop over breakfast and swore and sometimes admitted her into the overwhelming complexities of his life...

Then he'd head back into his bedroom/study or race to catch the ferry to Brisbane and she'd get on with her day, so there was no reason at all for her to feel different. Like there was a part of her that was starting to feel...grounded?

Like she had a home?

That was a crazy thought. It'd be gone in two years, she told herself, but still, the settled feeling persisted. And it grew, until she started to feel that something was changing, deep within. Something about the way he held her... Something about the way he made her feel...

And then, with this feeling growing stronger, one morning, when Angus was on call but things were quiet, when Seb had stayed overnight in Brisbane, when Freya was asleep at her feet after she'd taken her for an early morning swim...finally, finally, she sat down and started a letter.

Fifteen years ago, she'd given up her daughter for adoption. After an appalling birth, a time she only dimly remembered as a black hole of pain and terror, she'd held her baby for a whole ten minutes. Ten minutes and then she was gone.

She remembered feeling dazed, lost, helpless, and her aunt sitting by her bedside, spelling out the terms which had been negotiated by adults, her parents, the social workers, adults she didn't know.

'This adoption's through an intermediary agency, Jodie. The adoptive parents are required to report to the agency every six months, updating progress, but those updates stay with them. Because you're underage, your parents can access those updates for you, and you can access them yourself when you're of age, but there's to be no contact. However, when the child's eighteen, if she wishes, then she can approach you via the same agency. You might like to meet her then, if she wants to meet you.'

So why put out a tentative hope for contact now?

Why was Seb's arrival making her feel…as if she might have the strength to…just ask? To question her aunt's decree?

At fifteen, she hadn't had the courage to ask questions. She'd accepted what her aunt told her because she didn't have the strength to fight for what she couldn't cope with anyway. She'd had no resources. She'd had nothing.

And more, what she was left with, as Hali had disappeared into the unknown, was a shame so deep she could scarcely bear it. It wasn't her parents' shame she was left with though; it was her own. To bring a child into the world and then simply to discard her... How could she ever hope for contact? What if Hali looked at her with the contempt she deserved? What if she damaged the relationship with her now parents? Surely she had no right to try.

And so she'd built barriers, and she'd built them so carefully she'd thought they were impenetrable. But now... What was it about the way Seb held her, the way Seb hugged her before he left for Brisbane, that made her barriers feel like they were crumbling? All her barriers.

She didn't understand. All she knew was that for some reason she felt compelled to write—to the adoptive parents, via the agency.

I know this will seem out of the blue, and I understand if you and/or your daughter...

Her pen faltered over the words *your daughter*, but she made herself continue.

I understand if you and/or your daughter don't wish this, but if you could find it in your hearts to allow me to meet...

This was so hard. She crumpled the paper and tried again. And again.

Five attempts later, she had something that didn't make her cringe.

'Just do it,' she told herself, and Freya looked worriedly up at her and then nuzzled her hand. Like... 'We're in this together?'

'Yeah, you and me and Seb,' she whispered, and wondered why it seemed important—vital even—that Seb be part of this request.

Seb is not part of my life long-term, she told herself hastily. *But when he's holding me, within this makeshift marriage, I seem exposed anyway. So why not send the letter? And maybe, even if it's a blunt refusal, Seb will hold me in the night and make everything more bearable.*

Was that such a scary thought? Was she leaving herself far too exposed?

'You can do this,' she told herself out loud, but as she walked Freya along the beach track to the post office, she wondered whether she could try. In her relationship with her daughter?

In her relationship with Seb.

His gut hurt and it was getting worse.

Irritable bowel syndrome. That was what the physician he'd seen had told him more than once.

'Three bouts of dengue, Seb. I've never treated such a patient. Have you seen the list of drugs they used when you were fighting for life, in Al Delebe as well as here? It's enough to make your eyes water. I suspect the combination saved your life, but I imagine your gut's reacted exactly as it has. You know how long it takes for the gut flora to reestablish after even a short dose of antibiotics. Just give it time, Seb. And rest. Have you heard of rest?'

Yeah, right, as if he could rest. But he was sensible. He ate right, he took probiotics, he followed instructions...

Except rest. The legal complexities of taking control of Cantrell Holdings were enough to do his head in. Once the initial transfer had been sorted, he'd started transitioning to a leadership team to take the company in the direction he intended, but right now he felt responsible for everything.

He'd cut back on his media work as the face of the Al Delebe foundation. There was more than one reason for this. He seemed only to get voyeuristic questions about his marriage when he fronted the press, and he now had the funds to employ an excellent media team. But there were still mountains of foundation work to do behind the scenes, and he was damned if he'd give up his hands-on medicine.

His body was stretched to the limit.

The obvious thing to do would be to sleep solidly at night, he told himself, but there was the rub. At night, Jodie let him close, and how could a man resist that?

He wanted her, as simple as that. The more time he spent with her, the more he knew that, though the marriage might have started as fake, he wanted it to be real.

Why? She was lovely, desirable, tender, funny,

strong. Unbelievably, his great-uncle seemed to have chosen him the perfect bride.

But as well as her reservations—and he still didn't understand them—in his driven mind he had to accept that she was an indulgence. Time out from what really mattered. There was so much to do in the world, so many things he could change, and Jodie wasn't helping any of them.

That wasn't totally fair, he conceded. Without her agreeing to marry him he could have done nothing. Cantrell Holdings would have continued its path of ecological destruction. There'd have been no funds to continue the work in Al Delebe. Jodie had given him this.

But she hadn't…given. Not really. She'd accepted a cheque for a million dollars—heaven knew what she intended to do with it and it wasn't his business to ask. Maybe at the end of two years she'd leave medicine entirely and surf full-time.

He wouldn't be surprised. He was aware that she held herself distant, from her patients, from the islanders—and from himself.

Only at night did the rigid boundaries seem to crumble, but oh, the nights…

The nights where he sensed her longing to let go, to sink into him, to be…truly married.

How could he let that go in order to get the sleep his physician demanded?

He couldn't, but hell, his gut hurt.

CHAPTER ELEVEN

JODIE'S PHONE RANG at midnight.

She wasn't on call. She was, in fact, where she wanted to be more than anywhere else in the world. She was in Seb's arms, warm, safe, sated with loving. She was not on call, she told herself again, but Seb was already stirring, the ringing was continuous and she had to tug away.

Seb flicked on the bedside light as she answered, then lay back on the pillows, watching her.

He'd know this was trouble. Doctors' phones didn't ring at this hour except in need. Tonight, the after-hours calls should be directed to Angus's phone—he was officially on call—but the ID on the phone was... Angus?

This was definitely trouble.

'Jodie?'

'Yep.' She was sitting up now, the last vestiges of sated wonder falling away.

'A minibus has crashed.' Angus sounded distracted, and she could imagine him tugging on clothes as he spoke. 'Kids, camping at the end of the island. Overseas uni students. Seems they've been to the pub. I don't know who was driving— one of the kids? Surely not, but Les Irvine went home at the same time—he was at the pub too and saw them there. He was driving behind them and said the bus was weaving all over the road. He was already on the phone to Sergeant Cody when they went round the headland at Needle Bluff—and went straight over. Cody's on his way. Les is heading down the cliff now. He reckons there were maybe a dozen or more kids on the bus. It's fifteen, twenty feet down onto rocks. Can you come? And Seb? We're going to need everyone we can get.'

Seb was already swinging out of bed. Angus's voice had been loud and urgent, easily audible in the quiet of the bedroom.

A dozen kids. And she knew Needle Bluff. *Dear God...*

'We're on our way.'

The minibus had smashed its way down the rockface, landing on its side. By the time Jodie and Seb arrived, Les was already down the cliff. He must have seen their car lights and he shouted up to them, struggling to make his voice heard above the sounds of the surf.

'Track down twenty metres that-a-way. Jodie, you know it.'

Jodie obviously did. She turned to go left, holding one of the big torches they'd grabbed on the way out, but Seb gripped her hand, taking a moment to look down. To assess.

His work in Al Delebe had been mostly in the hospital, treating eye conditions, but medical facilities, medical help had been scarce. Often the team had been called to assist after accidents, or outbreaks of conflict, or any of the myriad disasters of a war-torn country. He'd therefore undertaken extra training in emergency medicine. He'd often had to deal with injuries far different to his specialist ophthalmology training, and some of those injuries had been dreadful.

And with that extra training, the DRABC code had been instilled almost as an instinct. Danger, Response, Airway, Breathing, Circulation.

Danger first. The moon was almost full. He could see, but he needed to know more.

'Tide?' he snapped. The minibus was on a rock ledge, and waves were washing up and over, already reaching the upturned bus.

And Jodie, who'd been tugging away from his hand, took a moment to think.

'It's coming in.'

'How fast?'

Jodie knew these waters, and how fast the tide was rising was vital knowledge in how much time they had to get the kids out. As they watched, they could see a kid struggling out through the smashed front window. Les was helping. There were already four kids out of the bus, sitting dazedly on the rocks.

'Maybe half an hour before it's in the bus,' she managed, and then caught herself and focused. 'No. The wind's from the south and it's building. Maybe less. And it'll take half an hour at least to get help from the mainland.'

'Then we get 'em out regardless,' he said grimly, feeling sick. If kids were trapped inside, knowing the tide was rising limited their options.

'Misty's rounding up locals,' Jodie told him. Angus had barked information to her before they'd ended the call. With a newborn and two other kids, Misty could hardly help, but she'd know the right islanders to call, the right emergency services on the mainland to contact. Angus had told her he was grabbing equipment from the clinic on his way, but for now Seb and Jodie were on their own.

Seb took one last glance down at the bus, using this higher vantage point to get a clearer idea of what they were facing. His hand tightened on Jodie's—but suddenly the hold became a hug. Fast but fierce. And then he moved on.

'We can do this,' he said simply. 'But the way the bus is lying… Why aren't more kids out? We might need to smash our way in to free them.' He took a swift glance around the area where they'd parked and grabbed a couple of thick pieces of timber from the undergrowth. He handed one to Jodie. 'Grab your bag,' he told her. 'Let's go.'

What followed was a nightmare. Sobbing, wounded—drunk?—kids seemed to have packed the minibus to capacity. By the time they reached the rock ledge, Les had six of them out through the smashed front windscreen. They seemed to be almost incapable of getting out themselves, with some, maybe the most wounded, blocking the way of others. But as Jodie stared in consternation at the scene before her, trying to figure where to start, Seb was suddenly in charge.

He'd held her up before they'd started down the track, and her instincts had screamed that they were wasting time. But as soon as they reached the bus he did a fast walk around, and now it seemed he had a plan. His voice reached out, not a yell, more like a sonic boom, sounding over the sobbing, the cries from inside the bus, the surf.

'Listen up. This is Dr Cantrell, Emergency Rescue.' That sounded official, Jodie thought, but she knew why he'd said it. These kids needed assurance that there were people in charge, people who knew what they were doing.

'We're coming in to get you out, but we need to break the rear window,' his booming voice continued. 'There's damage blocking it from opening so we need to smash it.'

He was playing his torch around the bus as he called, checking there was no one trapped underneath. Jodie did the same. Les had been helping kids out through one of the front windows, the only one that seemed both smashed and accessible, but now Seb's torch focused on the rear.

'We're about to break open the rear window,' he called, still in that amazing voice. Where had he learned to do this—it seemed loud enough to be heard from one end of the island to the other! But there was no panic behind it. 'Those still in the bus, turn away from the rear, and if anyone's trapped, I want them protected. I want faces covered from any debris coming in. Use your bodies if you must, to protect yourself and others. Right, everyone keep absolutely still. Now!'

Then he grabbed the stick Jodie was holding and handed it to Les. 'Sorry, love, but Les is stronger. You change to front window duty, helping anyone who can still access there.' His voice rang out again. 'Back window clear?'

'C-clear.' It was a quavering voice from within the bus, full of terror.

'Then hold still, everyone, and we'll clear a way to have you all free.'

There'd been thirteen kids on the bus. They got twelve of them out and, thankfully, among the kids being helped out of the wreckage, there seemed no critical injuries. There were lacerations, many of them deep. There were fractures. All these kids would need to be checked for internal damage, but for now there were no fatalities, and hopefully no injuries that meant death was likely.

By the time the twelfth kid was freed, Angus, Martin and as many capable islanders as Misty had been able to contact had joined them on the ledge. Floodlights were being set up and there were enough helpers to make the ledge crowded. It was growing even more crowded because the water was washing in.

Angus, Jodie and Martin were working as swiftly as they could, checking airways, stemming bleeding, trying to keep injured kids still, trying to calm rising hysteria. The least injured kids were being helped up the cliff, out of the range of the water. The tide was coming in at such a rate now, though, that the more seriously injured would need to be moved.

They needed choppers, stretchers, airlifts. They needed an army.

But in the minibus Seb needed a miracle. Someone other than him. There was one kid still in the van. One kid still trapped and the water was rising.

A girl. Eighteen? Nineteen? Trapped by the arm.

Cody was in the bus with him, the local cop, big, burly seemingly unflappable, following Seb's directions. Both of them were trying to ignore the rising water as they tried to shift crushed seats, struggling against whatever was holding the girl trapped. She seemed to be drifting in and out of consciousness, moaning for her mum, crying with pain and fear in her moments of consciousness.

Finally, the mangled seat that had been blocking their ability to figure what was holding her came away in Cody's hands. And Seb saw why they hadn't been able to tug her free.

Somehow, her arm was through the window. Trapped under the crushed side of the bus? *Dear God...*

Another wave washed through, two inches deep, maybe more. Another.

The girl's face was lying on metal. They couldn't lift her. They couldn't…

'We gotta lift the bus.' Cody's voice was grim as death, but Seb wasn't listening. He was lying full length on the metal frame of the bus, playing his torch over the trapped arm.

And what he saw… He felt sick. He pulled back, just a little but far enough so he could speak, softly but urgently, to the cop.

'Mate, it's half amputated already, and trying to move the bus—a team out there trying to lift, rocking it, the mess, the broken glass—if it slams back we'll kill her. We need airbags to slowly lift the whole bus, but there's no time, and all to save an arm that looks crushed beyond repair.' He took a deep breath, faced the inevitable—and then he moved on.

'Right. I need Jodie in here. Angus won't fit where I need him to be—Jodie's smaller.' He gave a mirthless laugh. 'Also, the last thing Jodie's scared of is a bit of seawater. I suspect even if we're submerged she'll just hold her breath and keep going. I'll need her for the anaesthetic. Tell her what's happening—between them, Angus and Jodie'll figure what I need.' And then, as another wave washed in, he said, 'Tell 'em fast.'

She wasn't an anaesthetist. She wasn't trained for this sort of crisis. Was anyone?

It seemed Seb was.

Anaesthetising a severely injured patient while lying in a wash of water among the chaos of a smashed bus was the stuff of nightmares, but Seb gave Jodie no time to indulge in fear.

'I've worked in a war-torn country for most of my life,' he told her simply. 'I'm no surgeon but I've faced this before.'

Part of her was horrified, but she didn't have time to ask more. From the moment she crawled through the chaos of twisted metal to reach him, he acted as though they were in Theatre already, scrubbed, ready to go. His calm voice implied this was normal, nothing out of the ordinary. His instructions were crisp, imbued with authority—infinitely reassuring in a situation that was anything but.

Before she'd crawled into the bus, she and Angus had done a fast think-through of what they'd need. There'd been no directions from Seb apart from that one passed-on order: 'Tell Jodie I need her as an anaesthetist for an amputation. Tell her I need everything.' Then Seb had simply assumed their competence, assumed the tools, the drugs he'd need would be there. And as she manoeuvred herself into the tiny space she needed to be in if she was to be of any use, as she tugged the bag of gear in after her, she thought he was assuming she was simply part of a team skilled in this sort of crisis.

Had he slipped back into war-torn Al Delebe?

But thank God for that, she thought, as she organised lights, a place to store the instruments they'd need out of reach of the water, as they talked fast and quietly of anaesthetic and risk. Of all the people to have...

She had a sudden flash of Seb as a kid. Living in a country where this sort of thing happened all the time.

They were working in a wash of seawater. Outside were the sounds of continuing chaos—the surf, the shouts of rescuers, the sobs of frightened kids. She could hear a helicopter above, maybe circling, trying to find a place to land.

Maybe a chopper would hold someone more qualified than her to help, she thought as the anaesthetic took hold, but then Seb's voice cut through.

'Ready? Block everything out, love, there's only this.'

And there was.

There was only Seb, and oh, thank God for him. The operation was appalling but they were fighting to save a life and there was no choice.

She couldn't have done it. She wouldn't have the skills, she wouldn't have the courage. But the alternative was to let the girl die.

And it seemed she did have the skills, or enough of the skills to support Seb's surgery. He simply assumed she was up for it—and maybe that was because he had no choice. She was all he had.

I'm all he has...

And at some time during that dreadful inter-lude, the phrase started echoing in her head.

She was all he had.

Right now, it was true, but it wasn't just now. He'd used her to prevent Cantrell Holdings con-tinuing its path of ecological destruction. He'd used her to keep the team in Al Delebe functioning.

And more.

He'd used her body to comfort him, to warm him, to give him strength when so many depended on him, when the weight of responsibility must seem almost impossible.

And now…the way he was working, the skill, the assurance, told her that horror had been part of his life. For ever?

And then she thought, what a privilege to be part of it. What a gift to be a partner to this man. To be a…helpmeet.

Helpmeet. The word was old-fashioned, used in the past in an almost derogatory sense. A man and his helpmeet.

This was her turf, though. Her island. This bus crash was her responsibility.

So, right now, she was a woman with a helpmeet.

She was working swiftly, handing implements, swabbing, making sure the lights were in the right place, adjusting her head lamp, the torches, to make sure his focus was where it needed to be. Working as hard as he was, doing the work of a team of theatre staff.

But no, she thought. She wasn't working as hard as he was. She didn't have the skills to save this girl. He had the skills—and the opportunity, she conceded—to save so many.

And when finally he pulled back, using his strength to pull the girl free, leaving the mangled arm where it lay, but finally able to hold her head above the rising water, when he said, in a voice that was curiously detached, 'Right, let's get her out of here,' she felt a wave of something so powerful she almost forgot to breathe.

He'd done this thing, but he'd done so much more besides. So much before.

And with that thought came more. She'd held herself back because she was afraid to commit. She'd held herself apart. Why?

She thought of the solitude of his life and she thought solitude had been her god. Was she utterly, totally selfish? Was she crazy?

She wanted to reach for him now, to hold him, to take the strained look from his face, to take as much of his burden as she could from his shoulders.

She couldn't—of course she couldn't. All she could do was back out of her crawl space, clamber out of the wreckage, leaving him holding his patient out of the water.

Outside there was chaos but it seemed the chaos was organised. There were paramedics from the chopper—they must finally have found a place to land. There were so many more. They were treating injured kids, but as she emerged, they all stilled. They'd been waiting for Seb—to save a life?

'He's done it,' she croaked, and her voice didn't come out right. There were so many emotions. 'She's free. If you could get the stretcher in there...'

And then Angus stepped forward and gave her a fierce hug—and she took it with relief and hugged back. She needed a hug.

She was a loner. She'd always been a loner. But right now the concept of being a loner seemed ridiculous. Seb was still in the bus, still working, still intent on saving a life. All around her were islanders, paramedics, a team of people all intent on doing just that.

No man is an island...

It was a quote from a poem. Donne, she thought, almost hysterically, and she remembered learning it in school as a fourteen-year-old, just before... just before Hali.

And then, after the drama, the pain, the fear surrounding the birth of her little girl, she remembered thinking of the same quote and deciding the poet was wrong.

No man is an island...

So now...she hugged Angus back and she thought, *Maybe Donne had it right all along?*

CHAPTER TWELVE

WHO KNEW WHAT the time was?

Who cared? She woke and sunbeams were streaming over the bed. It must be late, she thought dreamily, but it was more than late when she'd finally slept. The first rays of dawn had been creeping over the island as the last of the kids had been loaded onto the third medevac chopper and sent on their way to Brisbane.

There'd been no fatalities. There'd been broken bones, lacerations, things that would heal.

Or things that wouldn't. One lass would be facing a future without her left arm. Months of rehabilitation. A life that was changed for ever.

As was hers.

Instinctively, she reached out for Seb. Her bed had become their bed, a shared space where their precious independence had been put aside. What independence? It had been an illusion, she thought as the emotions, the self-knowledge of the night before flooded back.

'Seb,' she whispered and turned to touch him.

He wasn't there.

Blearily, she opened one eye and checked out the bedside clock. Eleven. Eleven?

Yikes.

Monday. It was Monday, she told herself. Monday was one of Seb's Brisbane days. Seriously, would he have risen at six and caught the ferry to the mainland? Was he so driven?

And once again the thought of his overwhelming responsibilities swept over her. How could one man keep on with such a load? And be alone.

Right now, she felt alone. She wanted him… here.

She just wanted him.

What was happening in the outside world? It felt surreal that she was lying in bed, soaking in the sunbeams washing over the bed, while Seb was somewhere in Brisbane—what, operating? Did he have a surgical list today? Or at one of his interminable company meetings as he struggled to get the control he needed?

Meanwhile, his wife lay in bed and thought, *Angus is rostered on for clinic this morning, and Misty will still be able to back him up if there's trouble. I can lie here for a while longer. Maybe I can go catch a wave?*

No. It felt deeply wrong.

Her whole life felt out of kilter.

Confused, she flung back the covers and headed out to the kitchen. And paused.

Usually, Seb had a fast breakfast before he headed out. This little house didn't run to a dishwasher, so he'd rinse his dishes and leave them on the sink. Also, he'd feed Freya and let her out.

But there were no dishes on the sink and Freya

was still on her bed by the stove. She wriggled her welcome as Jodie appeared, and then headed for the door. Fast. It seemed she'd been holding on. How early had Seb left? He must have been running for the ferry.

Jodie let her out. A letter lay on the veranda. Mail. Every islander would be doing what they could this morning, she thought, picking it up. Dot must have delivered this, thinking to spare her the walk down to the post office to collect it.

One letter. Formal. Buff envelope, almost the type a legal firm might send.

She double-checked the address, thinking legal letters were surely Seb's domain, but it was definitely hers. She sat on the back step, gave Freya a hug as she raced up for a pat and then slit the envelope.

Dear Ms Tavish
We're writing on behalf of the child you gave up for adoption on the...

Her heart seemed to just…stop. Her eyes were already starting to blur. She swiped unwanted, surely unnecessary, tears away with the back of her hand, and forced herself to read on.

It appears that Hali is eager to meet you, and her parents have signified their will-

*ingness to get in touch. If you're agreeable
they've suggested a possible meeting.*

*There's no compulsion for you to agree to
this, and if this raises concerns for you we
suggest you get in touch with our counsellor on...*

For long, long minutes she stared down at the
parchment, almost as if she was afraid it might
disintegrate in her hand.

Hali. Her Hali.

Oddly, the joy that suffused her first and foremost was that they hadn't changed her name. She
was still...her Hali?

Freya was now turning mad puppy circles in
front of her, anxious to share her morning ritual—
a piece of toast? But that was Seb's job, or rather
Seb's pleasure. A vet would have frowned him
down—dogs shouldn't eat human food—but Seb
had just laughed. 'Aren't we lucky there's no vet
on the island, hey, Freya?'

Seb. She rose and went inside to put bread in
the toaster, but her mind was in overdrive. This
letter. She wanted—no, she *needed* to show Seb.
She wanted to share.

Maybe she could go to Brisbane. Find him.

She had a sudden vision of seeing Hali...to-
gether? She'd need courage and Seb could...
would...give her courage.

Why would she need him?

Why *did* she need him?

She turned back to read the letter again, and there was such a jumble in her mind that she could hardly take it in. The emotions of the night before. The way Seb had held her when they'd finally showered and fallen into bed—they'd been exhausted beyond belief but still he'd held her. She'd gone to sleep in his arms, the nightmares of the night receding.

But she was a loner. Wasn't she?

What a lie.

And suddenly she found herself kneeling and hugging the big puppy tight, holding her as if her life depended on it. Confused but game, Freya did her canine best to hug back.

She'd never let anyone close. She'd never even let her dog close.

But why?

'Stupid, thy name is Jodie,' she whispered, thinking of the exhaustion on Seb's face, thinking of all he was facing, thinking of...her helpmeet.

Her lover.

Her husband.

'I need to find him,' she told Freya and rose but, to Freya's disapproval, she didn't move across to the bench to fetch the toast. Instead, she headed for the bathroom. She needed to dress. If she had to go to Brisbane to find him then so be it.

'Toast'll have to wait,' she called back over her

shoulder. 'Sorry, Freya, love, I need to find…my other love.'

And then she tugged open the bathroom door— and there he was.

Seb.

He was slumped on the bathroom floor. Unconscious. Lying in a pool of blood.

Dear God…dead?

He wasn't dead. Those first frantic seconds as she knelt, as she fought to find a pulse, as panic almost overwhelmed her, would live with her for ever.

What…? How…?

Think. As she found his pulse, thready but racing, as she realised life was still there, she had to fight with everything she possessed to put herself in doctor mode. What she wanted to do was to tug him into her arms and wail. Somehow, she managed to sit back, force back panic and assess.

Blood. He'd been vomiting blood? Bright blood, fresh. He hadn't been here for long then. But so much blood.

Dear God, what?

Instinctively, she was clearing his airway, tugging him into recovery position, her mind racing.

What? What?

Vomiting blood. Stomach ulcer? Malignancy? Oh, God, the fear of that.

Don't go down that path, she told herself, panic surging again.

He looked ashen. Grey. How much blood had he lost?

Far too much.

She needed help. Now. Angus. Misty.

It took every shred of strength she had to get off the floor and run.

Freya met her at the door—she'd been promised toast and she wasn't a dog to forget. Get her outside. She grabbed the toast, opened the back door and hurled it into the backyard. Two slices—more than a dog could possibly hope for—but as Freya bounded after the toast she paused, just for a second, to look back. Almost as if she was figuring there was something else a dog should do. Something was wrong?

And Jodie gave an almost hysterical laugh. She had her phone and was already waiting for Angus to answer.

'Jodie?'

'It's Seb.' She wasted no words. 'Possible gastric bleed. Massive blood loss. Unconscious. I need help. Medevac but blood. Do we have plasma expander?'

There was a sharp intake of breath. 'We used it all last night,' he told her. She could hear Misty in the background, her voice sharp with concern.

'I guess… IV saline…' Her mind was refusing to work. With this much blood loss, if they didn't restore pressure… No, that was unthinkable.

And then Misty was on the line. 'Jodie, Angus

is grabbing gear and he's on his way. I'll ring Brisbane and organise medevac. Ben Roberts and Sylvia and Donna Marchant are O negative and Martin'll dredge up records to see if we have more. Universal donors—I know they'll help and we can do it faster than it'll take medevac to arrive. We'll call them in now. Go back to him and hold on.'

What followed was the worst few hours of Jodie's life.

What followed was the realisation of just how deeply, how completely, how absolutely she loved him.

When she thought she might lose him.

The IV lines weren't enough. Mere fluid wasn't enough to increase blood pressure for long, and for a few appalling minutes it became almost unrecordable. For those awful minutes she expected the worst at any minute—that Seb's heart would simply fail.

How long had he been there? Why hadn't he called her? He must have felt appalling, must have had the strength to get to the bathroom.

He hadn't woken her because...

Because he was a loner? Or because she was. Because she'd made it absolutely clear they didn't depend on each other, that they stayed apart.

Oh, God, how long would help take to arrive?

She and Angus were fighting with everything they had. How long before the medevac chopper could arrive with life-saving blood expander? How long before they could get him to Brisbane? How long before skills were needed that neither she nor Angus possessed?

But then, before she thought it possible, Dot, the postmistress, was calling from the kitchen, 'Blood—Misty and Martin have a queue at the clinic lined up to donate. This is the first but they'll have more. We're bringing it in as it comes.'

Jodie went into the kitchen to receive it—it seemed more important to her that Angus stayed, because surely he was more skilled than she was. Surely someone had to be.

And as Dot handed her the bag she looked at Jodie, bloodstained, white-faced and grim, and she reached out and gave her a hug.

'He'll be fine, love,' she said in a voice that was none too steady. 'Seb has the whole island behind him, and so do you. Every single islander's wishing they were O negative now. You're not alone, girl, and if people power means anything, then he'll be just fine.'

CHAPTER THIRTEEN

SEB WOKE AND he was surrounded by tubes, by lights, by beeping machines, by glowing screens. Where?

He'd been in enough hospitals to figure it out, though it took him a few moments. Intensive Care. ICUs the world over were terrifying places. There was no way they could be made cosy and personal. They were set up to save lives.

His eyes had flicked open for just long enough to take it in, but now he closed them again, trying to recall… Trying to figure…

Pain. Fear. Blood.

Nothing.

Someone was holding his hand.

'Seb?' It was a whisper.

Jodie. That was enough for him to force his eyes open again, fighting a fog that seemed to be trying to envelop him. 'J…' His mouth wouldn't work. His head wouldn't work.

'I'm here,' she whispered, and her face was on his cheek, her hair a faint whisper brushing his skin. And then the lightest of kisses—and a quiet sob.

Jodie was crying. What? He had to surface; this was important. Nothing was more important than Jodie crying.

But her hand was on his face, lightly cradling, her fingers on his lips.

'Don't try and talk, love. You're safe. Duodenal ulcer, a bleed, a big one. But we…we got you here, to Brisbane Central. You've been in surgery. You're all patched up.' Here her voice broke again and he heard tears behind the words. 'You tried…you must have woken and tried…to cope alone. That's never going to happen again, I swear. Never. I'll cling like a limpet. Seb, I love you so much. I'll love you…for ever.'

It was too much. No, it wasn't too much. His eyes closed again because it seemed he had no choice, but somehow his hand groped and found hers. Fingers intertwined and clung. The feel of her…the strength of her…

For some reason, the years of bleakness were washing through him. A childhood where his parents had loved him but were so caught up in their careers, their passion for caring for others, that he had to be an outsider. Then the years of joining them in their care, of considering every other moment was wasted. The work, the passion, the time…

But now…this. Maybe for this moment he could just…

'For ever, Seb,' Jodie whispered, and her lips brushed his. 'I've made a vow and I've realised… if you want me to break that vow, I'll fight you every inch of the way. I love you, Seb Cantrell, and whatever it takes, I'll love you for ever.'

* * *

Doctors look after their own. Seb was a Brisbane Central specialist and Jodie was a referring doctor. She was therefore shown to a tiny apartment used for doctors on call. That meant that if anything happened—the merest hiccup—she could be with Seb in minutes.

But his body was so debilitated. For those first days, as complication after complication set in, even though he was barely conscious, even though there was nothing she could do, she hardly left his side.

For four long days his life seemed to hang in the balance. For days the haematologists, the gastroenterologists, the cardiologists were in and out, adjusting, working, doing their damnedest to pull him out of the woods.

Seb's normal treating doctor, the tropical diseases specialist, was there as well, efficient, clinical, but deeply concerned. And on day four, when blood counts finally started to stabilise, when his heart rate finally settled, when finally, finally the treating team was starting to relax, the man even apologised to Jodie.

'It's a trap,' he said grimly. 'The dengue fever was such a big flag. Polyarthralgia, myalgia, joint and muscle pain, plus ongoing fatigue, they're known long-term after-effects of dengue. Seb and I both know that, and we haven't looked any further. But the duodenal ulcer…after the treatments he's undergone, the effects on every part of his body, hell, we should have looked further.'

'And I'm betting he didn't ask you to look,' she told him, and fought to keep the quaver from a voice she needed to imbue with steel. 'He's been too busy. So, so busy. Well, that's about to change.'

'Really?' He eyed her curiously. 'You know how important his work is?'

'It's not important at all if he's dead,' she retorted. 'So that's my priority. To keep him alive.'

And the doctor's face softened. 'You must have been terrified. I'm so sorry.' He hesitated and then added, 'The doctors here have told me you've hardly slept yourself. You must love him very much.'

'Not nearly as much as I'm going to love him,' she said fiercely—and then she burst into tears.

And then, ten days after he was admitted, he was finally discharged. Into her care.

Misty and Angus came over from the island to help Jodie take him home. 'That'll leave the island without doctors,' he'd protested when they'd told him, but Misty had dismissed his protests out of hand.

'Martin's there, but I think the islanders are too busy getting things ready to worry about getting sick.'

Getting things ready? He didn't understand but then, he was still feeling dazed. The surgery, the ongoing treatment, had knocked the stuffing out of him—or maybe the stuffing had been knocked out of him a long time ago. It was only now, when Jodie was watching every move he made, when he was surrounded by a medical team that was not only skilled but also deeply concerned about him as a person, that he'd decided to let things go. To let other people worry.

To take the care and be grateful.

To take Jodie's love?

There was so much he still didn't understand. Jodie, who'd stood apart from him for the whole time he'd known her, who'd sworn she needed no one, was suddenly fiercely with him.

His wife.

She'd decided she loved him? In truth, he hardly knew how to accept such a gift. All he knew for now was that it seemed a gift without price. Unconditional. Absolute.

He'd figure it out in time, he decided when the daze of illness receded, when the effects of shock and drugs wore off—when he got home.

Home to the island. Home to Freya.

Home with Jodie.

Leaving the hospital turned out to be almost a ceremony in itself. He hadn't realised how many of the staff knew him, and many of the team members managed to be in the corridors, in the foyer, out on the entrance ramp as he left. He'd been offered a wheelchair, which he'd scorned, but he was grateful for Jodie's arm. Very grateful.

He couldn't manage this alone.

And Misty and Angus were right behind.

'I've read your history,' Misty told him when he protested. 'How many things have you had wrong with you, Seb Cantrell? Angus and Jodie and I have decided to split your rehab. I'm in charge of exercise. At post-partum, our exercise regime should pretty much match. As of tomorrow, you and I both get to tie each other's shoelaces. How about that for a plan?'

He grinned and subsided, and now, as Jodie held him, as Angus and Misty followed, as the medics of Brisbane Central cheered his farewell, he felt…

That these were his people. This was his place.

His life.

The ferry felt the same. A place had been reserved for him in the front of the boat. The crew offered cushions, blankets and enough care to make a man revolt—but their eagerness to help couldn't be rejected. He allowed himself to savour it, and the emotions within grew and grew.

When he arrived, there were islanders at the terminal, hugging Jodie, not hugging him but clearly wanting to, hugging Angus and Misty instead. Hugging each other.

And then finally they were home. There were people at their front gate. Someone had been holding Freya. She was released and surged forward to greet them. Angus caught her before she jumped, but Jodie was on her knees, hugging the dog, eyes misty with tears.

'She's been staying with us,' Misty told them. 'You want her to stay with us for another few days?'

'She stays here,' Seb growled, struggling against tears himself. 'Home.'

Misty smiled and hugged the dog herself. Then she and Angus escorted them to the door, gestured them in, dropped their bags in the porch and closed the door behind them.

Home.

He stood for a moment, still holding Jodie's hand, trying to come to terms with a mass of emotion so huge he could hardly take it in.

'Home, love,' Jodie whispered, and he tugged her around and kissed her, a kiss that was long, deep, sure. There were things he didn't understand, things he needed to figure, but all he knew now was that she was here. His Jodie. His wife.

When they finally surfaced, he saw she'd lost the struggle with tears. She swiped them away and turned, seemingly overwhelmed.

'Oh, for heaven's sake,' she managed. 'The islanders have been here.'

He turned and looked. The little cottage looked super clean, super bright. Freya was sniffing round, obviously checking out new smells. There were containers on the bench—he could see cakes, biscuits in clear plastic containers. A massive bunch of flowers took centre stage on the table.

'Oh, my heaven!' Jodie walked forward and opened the fridge, and its contents almost fell out at her. So much love was being shown by so much food. 'There's enough for an army here. Seb, look!'

But Seb was distracted. There were a couple of notes on the table. One, a card, had obviously come with the flowers.

To Drs Seb and Jodie,
Please accept these as a tiny token of our gratitude for your role in saving our daughter's life.

Beth's recovering well. It'll take time to come to terms with the loss of her arm, but she accepts how appalling the alternative was. The doctors here have spelt out that alternative—and they've also described the skills needed to amputate in such circumstances.

Dr Jodie's already visited and made an offer of surfing lessons as soon as Beth's up for it. She says who needs two arms for surfing? And for some reason that's given Beth more hope than we can convey.

So, to both of you... There are simply no words to express our thanks.

'You've been in touch with Beth?' he said wonderingly.

'She was in the same hospital,' she retorted, her head still in the fridge. 'You kept sleeping. What else was a woman to do? Wow, beef bourguignon. That's dinner settled.'

Her voice was rough, almost embarrassed, and he thought, *Is she retiring into her shell again? Jodie?* There was so much he didn't understand.

And then he picked up the second letter. It was formal, typed. And before he'd realised it was addressed to Jodie, he'd scanned the first couple of lines.

Dear Ms Tavish
We're writing on behalf of the child you gave up for adoption on the...

It wasn't his letter. This was none of his business. He pushed the letter aside as if it burned, and looked at Jodie.

Who was looking at him.

And on her face...fear?

'I'm sorry.' She reached forward and snatched the letter, crumpling it. 'I didn't... It's just... Oh, the islanders will have seen it.'

'I'm sorry.' He hesitated and then said softly, 'Jodie, it's your letter, but I can't unsee it.'

'I didn't want...'

'Anyone to know you have a child?'

'I don't have a child.'

'But you…*had* a child?' His voice softened still further, sounding each syllable with care. 'A girl? A boy?'

'A daughter.' The distress on her face was obvious, a warring of emotion. 'My daughter. My Hali.'

'Hali?'

'It means the sea. Greek mythology. I was really into mythology when I was fifteen.'

'Fifteen.' He felt as if all the air had been sucked out of him. He was watching her face, seeing her distress, and feeling as if some giant jigsaw puzzle was suddenly assembling before his eyes. 'You had Hali when you were fifteen?'

'I don't want to talk about it.'

'Why not?' he asked gently and she shook her head.

'I don't know. I… Tea? Cake? There seems to be enough.'

'Tea and cake would be great,' he said gravely and sat and watched her as she collected mugs and boiled the kettle and then seemed to take a great deal of time choosing which of the cakes to bring to the table.

Sponge cake with what looked like raspberry filling and icing? Great choice. He sat and watched her slice and serve, but then hesitate. He had the feeling she wanted to run, but of course there was no choice. This was where they lived. This was their life.

And finally, she sat. And stared at the table.

The letter was still in her hand. Crumpled. She'd made tea, she'd served cake without letting it go.

'I suspect your letter's precious,' he said, feeling as if he was making his way through a minefield. 'You might like to put it away before you get raspberry cream on it.'

'I… Everyone's seen it.' Her words were flat, dull, filled with pain. 'I just… I'd just opened it when you…'

'When you found me.' The cake, the tea, lay untouched in front of them. 'Jodie…a daughter. That's huge. Could you find it…could you find it in you to tell me?'

She closed her eyes, took a deep breath and then handed the letter over to him.

'You want me to read it?'

'I… Yes.'

He hesitated for a long moment, and then read and reread. When he looked up, Jodie's eyes were fixed on him, her expression unreadable.

'Have you had no contact?'

'I couldn't… I couldn't bear to. I had no right.'

There was so much behind that statement it took his breath away.

'Do you want to know about her now?' he asked tentatively, but he didn't have to finish the question. Her eyes blazed with such intensity that he knew. In that look…longing, hurt, need, the ache of a loss past bearing…

'Tell me,' he said, his eyes not leaving her face. 'If you can.'

She winced and stared down at the crumpled letter. 'Nothing to tell,' she muttered. 'Sordid little story. Kids on the beach late at night, a fumble in the dark that got out of hand, a teenage pregnancy.'

'At fifteen?' He closed his eyes. 'I can't imagine. Your parents?'

She gave a hollow laugh. 'I wasn't their daughter. I never had been, not really. They tried really hard to have a baby and then they had their daughter, Joy. She died at birth. So they adopted me but I was never… Joy. I was their duty. Everything I did…well, I just wasn't Joy.'

'Oh, love…'

She shrugged. 'Enough. They did their duty by me but we weren't close. Anyway, I was dumb. I didn't even realise I was pregnant—or maybe I did, I just blocked it out until I was six months gone when my gym teacher guessed and phoned my mother. And then…' She closed her eyes. 'I remember… I came home from school and she hauled me to the doctor and then there was this interminable weekend where they wouldn't even talk to me. They were…well, they were committed to a religion that pretty much told them I was a whore. So, on the Monday, instead of school they packed me into the car and drove me to Melbourne. To my aunt's.'

'Your aunt.' He hesitated, trying to think this through. Trying to imagine himself in her place. 'Hell. Was she good to you?'

'You're kidding. She was as puritanical as my parents. I was the fallen woman and I gather… I learned later that they paid her.'

'Oh, love…'

She shook her head. 'It didn't matter. I coped. I buried myself in my books and my…unreality. My parents didn't even come when…when Hali was born. A thirty-six-hour labour and then a Caesarean. And then, while I was still so fuzzy, there was talk and talk and talk, my aunt talking at me, about what was best for the baby, about what was the only course, talking about the disgrace I'd brought to my parents, and I knew I had no support, no way to keep her. I guess…there was just no one. So she was adopted and I was enrolled in boarding school. I never went home—my parents couldn't bear the shame. From then on, I spent my holidays with my aunt. There was nothing left for me but…but study. Oh, and surfing. I could catch a bus from my aunt's—an hour to the nearest surf but it was worth it. I was a loner but that was okay. No one judged me while I surfed.'

'Jodie!' This was like something out of a nightmare. Did parents really react like this? How could they?

Jodie's face said it was all too real.

'Afterwards, I tried to ask for contact,' she whispered, speaking almost to herself. 'But of course I was too young to push past barriers I didn't understand, too young to even know how to go about it, and the things I apparently signed...' She shrugged. 'By the time I realised I could fight it, I wondered what right I had to mess with a life I didn't deserve. But then...somehow...' She hesitated and for the first time she looked directly at him. 'A few weeks back it suddenly seemed like I might try again.'

And there was something in her face...

'Because of us?' It was hardly a whisper.

And her eyes filled with tears. 'Maybe,' she managed. 'Maybe I realised I didn't want to be a loner any more. Maybe...maybe I found the courage not to be?'

And then he was out of the chair, around the table, kneeling before her. Hell, he hadn't realised he could kneel. Probably it hurt—who cared, who even noticed? But he was cupping her face in his hands, searching her eyes, seeing...truth.

'Because of us?' he asked again, because it was so important.

'Seb, I don't want... I never thought... I don't need you.'

'Really?' he murmured and there was something in his heart that said this was right, this was true. And with that thought so much fell away. Priorities that had been instilled since birth.

Surely love needed to come first. Surely everything else could follow. This was Jodie.

His love.

'Then that's a shame,' he said softly, 'because I sure as hell need you.' He was looking into her eyes, seeing what he must have known all along. That this woman was strong, true, wonderful. This woman was a woman in a million. This was the woman he wanted to spend his life getting to know.

'Jodie.' It was all he could do to get his voice to work but this was important. So important. 'Why did you agree to marry me?'

'Because of your work,' she murmured. 'I knew how much it meant.'

'So the million…'

'It's already given away.'

'What…?'

'There's an organisation, set up in rural Queensland, supporting young mums, helping them keep their babies if they want. Giving them mothering skills. Helping with their continued education.' She took a deep breath. 'With my million… Okay, it's a drop in the ocean, but it's not only you who'd like to save the world, Seb Cantrell. But we can't keep on. *You* can't keep on. You'll kill yourself. Surfing saved me. What's going to save you?' She took a deep breath, swiped more tears away and took a deep breath.

'Seb, I love you. I've figured that out and it's… it's changed my world. But I can't watch you kill yourself with what you're trying to achieve. I've spent fifteen years not needing anyone. I'm damned if I'll…'

'Jodie,' he said, very softly now. 'Shut up.'

She tugged back a little, her expression changing. 'What?'

'I love you too.'

'You…' She shook her head. 'You can't. There'll be someone…more worthy…'

'You're kidding me, right? A woman better than you? A woman who's had a baby when you were too young to cope, but who's managed just fine. Who's faced down her parents' cruel judgements. Who's coped with love and loss, who's built a career, who's become a surfer with skills so extraordinary she even teaches. A woman who dives into rocky surf to save a geriatric megalomaniac without even thinking. A woman who crawls into smashed buses and helps me save lives. You're a… what? You're a woman in a million.' He paused and frowned. 'Jodie, have you answered that letter?'

'I… No.' She was thrown off-kilter. 'I…'

'You received it ten days ago and it's lain on the table ever since. You ignored it…'

'I didn't ignore it. At least…' She shook her

head, almost wonderingly. 'I forgot about it,' she confessed.

'You forgot the most important thing?'

'I… It wasn't the most important thing. You were dying.'

'I didn't die.' He grinned then, and everything was suddenly in its right place. He was kneeling before the woman he loved with all his heart. Everything else—his medicine, Al Delebe, Cantrell Holdings—they needed to fit around this, he thought, and it was suddenly a vow. It would take more delegating, more trust, more determination, but if he didn't have Jodie…if he didn't share her life as well as asking her to share his…

And with that knowledge came the certainty that he'd have to step back. Changing the world was all very well, but Jodie was part of that world.

No. Right now, it seemed that Jodie *was* his world.

'Jodie, will you marry me?' It was a simple request, said humbly, said with such love, such conviction that even Freya, nosing around under the table—she could smell cake—paused and raised her head to listen. It seemed the whole world was hanging on these next few moments.

'Seb…'

'Really marry, I mean,' he said, and there was urgency in his voice. 'You married me the first time so my world could continue. Now, I'm asking if I can be part of your world. Yes, the work I do is important, but surely it can be delegated. Part of that will mean sharing my life with you. And me sharing your life. Living on this island, meeting your daughter, training Freya, learning to surf—because hell, there's no way you can keep that to yourself, I want—no, I *need* to share that as well. It's going to be tricky. There'll be so much we need to work out, but if we can…for now, please, Jodie, will you marry me?'

There was a long, long silence. His hands were cupping her face. She was looking into his eyes and there were so many questions, so many answers, silently spoken in that gaze.

And finally, blessedly, wonderfully, she smiled, her eyes brimming with unshed tears.

'Yes,' she said, but her voice was muffled with emotion.

It didn't matter, for after that there was no need for words for a very long time.

A wedding. A man, a woman and two witnesses, or three if you counted a dog—Misty and Angus and Freya—but no one else. A simple ceremony in the island chapel, because it seemed that this time the vows needed to be made in a place where such vows felt sacrosanct. But these were simple vows, made to each other, with no need for priest or celebrant.

There were no costumes this time. No finery. The bride wore shorts and a simple white blouse.

Her legs were bare, her hair free and flowing. The groom wore chinos and a casual shirt. The bride carried a tiny bouquet of wattle, picked that morning from their cottage garden. The groom had attached a sprig to his shirt.

'I, Jodie, take thee, Seb, to love and to honour, from this day forward…'

'I, Seb, take thee, Jodie, to love and to honour, from this day forward…'

These were vows meant only for each other. These were vows that would last a lifetime.And then, as Angus and Misty beamed mistily and held tightly to Freya, who was threatening to surge forward and show her own appreciation, as the flautist Misty had sneaked into the church vestry piped a simple, perfect version of Ed Sheeran's *Perfect*, as the vows they made echoed and faded into the walls of the sunlit chapel, Seb Cantrell and Jodie Tavish smiled at each other and then walked hand in hand out into the sunshine. To begin the rest of their lives.

EPILOGUE

IT WAS DONE. She'd arranged to meet her daughter.

After that first letter Jodie had written back, offering to go to her, to meet wherever they suggested. But, amazingly, Miriam and Bob Holt had replied saying they lived in one of Brisbane's outer suburbs and would love an excuse to take the ferry across to Kirra Island.

'Let's make it informal,' Miriam had suggested. 'We could bring a picnic, go the beach? Hali's very tense, but if she could tie in a swim it might help break the ice. She has a little brother, adopted four years after Hali, and they both love the sea. If they could play in the surf, make it mostly about fun, meeting you might not feel so nerve-racking?'

It was a good idea, but for Jodie there was no way the day could be anything but nerve-racking. But Seb was beside her and so was Freya. They'd checked to make sure there were no family allergies, but it seemed no one was allergic to dogs. No one was allergic to anything.

So on a gorgeous Saturday afternoon, a month after their true wedding, Seb and Jodie headed to one of Kirra's most beautiful beaches and settled down to wait.

They had offered to meet the ferry, but there was no way six people and a dog could fit in the beach buggy—maybe one day they'd need to do something about that? So Jodie and Seb had driven to the beach alone, and Mack was under instructions to collect and deliver…whoever came.

The taxi pulled up right on time. Jodie walked up the track to meet it—and came face to face with her daughter.

Hali. Fifteen years old. Blonde, skinny, freckled. Tall for her age. Trying to smile through nerves. Behind her were her parents and a kid brother, smiling nervously as well.

'I guess…you must be my birth mum,' the girl managed, because Jodie was clearly unable to say anything at all. And then she gave her a shy smile. 'I've wanted to meet you. We've all wanted to, for a long time.' She waved across to her brother, a gangly kid, all arms and legs. 'Josh met his birth mum when he was eight. She wasn't much interested though. Why didn't you want to meet me until now?'

Trust a teenager to get right to the point. This was such a huge question.

In her imagination, Jodie had thought this could take many meetings, maybe with a counsellor present, someone professional to unpack the emotional baggage threatening to overwhelm her. But she had Seb and Freya. Seb was by her side and his hand was gripping hers, warm and strong, and Freya was nosing forward, sniffing Hali, and Hali was stooping to pat her.

Miriam and Bob were standing back, letting their…their daughter…take the lead. Both of them were smiling.

And finally, Jodie found her voice. 'I didn't know how to,' she managed. 'Hali, I was so scared. I had you three days after I turned fifteen—that's younger than you are now—and I didn't know what to do. I… I didn't have parents who loved me. I felt alone and frightened and all I knew was that… I wanted you to have parents who loved you. Parents who wouldn't let you be alone and frightened. And Hali…until now I didn't feel… I didn't feel old enough or brave enough to follow through. I was so ashamed that I couldn't keep you. That I couldn't care for you. I didn't even feel like I had the right to have a daughter.'

What followed was a long silence, where Hali seemed to take this on board and consider. Everyone seemed to hold their breath as Hali surveyed Jodie from head to foot—until finally she seemed to come to a decision. And, teenager-like, her decision was blunt.

'That's cool,' she said, and then she said tentatively, 'And my…birth father?'

'He was a kid too. I haven't kept in touch, but he knows about you. If you want, maybe we can figure out a way…'

'You didn't love him?'

'I was a kid, Hali. I didn't…' Deep breath. 'I didn't know what love was.'

'But you know now?'

That was easy. Seb was right here—and she was here for Seb.

'I do,' she said, and it was a vow all on its own.

But Hali was losing interest. 'Fair enough,' she said, but she was now looking around the cove. She saw the sea glistening through the palms, she saw the golden sand—and she saw Seb and Jodie's surfboards, which were permanently on the roof of their buggy.

'Do you surf?' she demanded.

'I do,' Jodie said again.

'I never have,' Hali said wistfully. 'And you?' She turned to Seb. 'Do you both surf?'

'I don't surf very well,' Seb admitted, and Jodie felt him tug her close. 'But Jodie's teaching me.' He hesitated, looking from Jodie to Hali and back again, then seemed to come to a decision. 'Jodie's the best teacher. If we can organise it, maybe she can teach you?'

'And me?' Josh piped up eagerly from the background. 'We're family. If you're going to teach Hali, then you have to teach me.'

'Fair enough,' Seb said, grinning, as Jodie's insides seemed to turn to mush. Was this what it meant for a heart to melt? And then, as Seb kissed her lightly, then released her to untie the boards from the buggy, her heart melted even more.

'I guess it's just the way things are,' he was saying. 'Family... Isn't it where we find it? And how lucky are we that we have?'

* * * * *

If you enjoyed this story, check out these other great reads from Marion Lennox

Baby Shock for the Millionaire Doc
Her Off-Limits Single Dad
Healed by Their Dolphin Island Baby
Dr. Finlay's Courageous Bride

All available now!